HELP!

I'M TRAPPED IN MY
CAMP COUNSELOR'S BODY

Other books by Todd Strasser

Help! I'm Trapped in an Alien's Body

Help! I'm Trapped in Obedience School Again

Help! I'm Trapped in Santa's Body

Help! I'm Trapped in the First Day of Summer Camp

Camp Run-a-Muck series:

#1: Greasy Grimy Gopher Guts

#2: Mutilated Monkey Meat

#3: Chopped Up Little Birdy's Feet

Help! I'm Trapped in My Sister's Body

Help! I'm Trapped in the President's Body

Help! I'm Trapped in My Gym Teacher's Body

Howl-A-Ween

Help! I'm Trapped in Obedience School

Abe Lincoln for Class President

Help! I'm Trapped in the First Day of School

Please Don't Be Mine, Julie Valentine

Help! I'm Trapped in My Teacher's Body

The Diving Bell

Free Willy (novelization)

Jumanji™ (novelization)

Home Alone™ (novelization)

Home Alone™ *II: Lost in New York* (novelization)

The Mall from Outer Space

HELP!
I'M TRAPPED IN MY
CAMP COUNSELOR'S BODY

TODD STRASSER

AN
APPLE
PAPERBACK

SCHOLASTIC INC.
New York Toronto London Auckland Sydney

ISBN 0-590-03272-0

12 11 10 9 8 7 6 5 4 3 2 1   8 9/9 0 1 2 3/0

Printed in the U.S.A.   40

First Scholastic printing, June 1998

To Emily, Adam, and Lucy Wickersham

HELP!

I'M TRAPPED IN MY
CAMP COUNSELOR'S BODY

NOTE

Hi, it's me, Jake Sherman, the kid who's always switching bodies with other people. I know that my stories sometimes get sort of funny, but before you read this book, I need to talk to you about something serious.

Everybody makes mistakes. No one likes to admit it, but we all goof up now and then. The truth is, even good, smart people sometimes make bad, dumb mistakes. They don't mean to, but, hey, it happens.

I just think that maybe we're a little too hard on people who make mistakes. Maybe we ought to lighten up when someone we know blows it big time.

Because next time it might be our turn to mess up. And we don't want people coming down hard on us for an honest mistake, do we?

Believe me, I know what I'm talking about.

PART ONE
THE ULTIMATE MESS-UP

1

"At least it's not lamb brain tacos," said my friend Josh Hopka. "They're considered a delicacy in Mexico. Or sun-dried maggots. They love 'em in China."

It was the day before summer vacation, and my friends and I were eating lunch in the cafeteria. On the last day at Burt Ipchupt Middle School, they always served us something called Last Day Surprise.

This year it was a stew with greenish pieces of celery, chunks of potato, thin white strips of chicken, and orange disks of carrot, all floating in a light-colored sauce.

"Maybe it's chicken pot pie without the pie," I guessed, staring down at my plate.

"Or chicken chow mein without the rice," said my friend Andy Kent.

"For all we know, it could be yesterday's garbage without the flies," Josh added cheerfully.

"But at least it's not coconut-cream-marinated dog."

Josh had gotten a book of gross-outs from the school book fair and now at lunch he insisted on reading these disgusting recipes. He flipped to another page. "Maybe it's white ant pie, a very popular meal in Tanzania."

"Chill, Josh," I said. "You're starting to gross us out."

"Sure, Jake," Josh taunted me. "You'd want something easier to digest. Like broiled beetle grubs from Japan or maybe cooked baked bat from Samoa."

"That's a redundancy," Andy pointed out.

"A what?" I asked.

"It means Josh said something twice that he only had to say once," Andy explained. "He said baked so he didn't have to say cooked."

Josh made a face. "What's with you?"

"It's that English final we had this morning," Andy explained. "I can't get that stuff out of my head. Anyway, guys, just think, we're halfway through our last day of school."

Outside the trees were covered with new green leaves and kids were walking around in T-shirts and shorts.

"Yeah," said Josh as he speared a carrot with his fork and raised it toward his mouth. "And as bad as this lunch is, it probably beats what we'll be eating at that new camp Jake picked."

4

"No way," I protested. "Didn't you guys watch the video the camp sent?"

Josh and Andy shook their heads.

"My parents were too busy," Josh said. "They said if the camp was good enough for your parents, it had to be okay."

"And we got so many videos, after a while we gave up watching them," Andy said. "My dad says all camp videos are the same. They all show lakes and waterfronts."

"And ball fields and basketball courts," added Josh.

"And camp-outs with kids roasting marshmallows and singing dumb camp songs," said Andy.

"Seen one, seen 'em all," Josh concluded.

"Not the camp I picked for us *this* year," I said proudly.

2

I was just about to tell my friends about our new camp when Mr. Dirksen came by.

"Jake, could you come to the science lab with me?" he asked. "Something urgent has come up and I must speak with you."

Mr. Dirksen was our science teacher and the inventor of the Dirksen Intelligence Transfer System, or DITS.

"Uh, sure." I got up and looked at my friends. "Catch you later, guys."

Mr. Dirksen and I left the cafeteria and started down the hall to the science lab.

"What are your plans for the summer, Jake?" he asked.

"My friends and I are going to camp again," I answered as we pushed open the door to the science lab.

Inside was the DITS. It was a fairly large invention consisting of a computer terminal and two lounge chairs. Mr. Dirksen had originally invented

6

it with the idea of transferring knowledge from one person to another. But all it really did was make people switch bodies.

"Are you going to leave the DITS here in school for the summer?" I asked.

"That one, yes," answered Mr. Dirksen as he closed the lab door behind him.

"That one?" I scowled. "I thought there was only one DITS."

Mr. Dirksen gave me a jaunty smile. "Can you keep a secret, Jake?"

"Sure."

"I assumed you could," Mr. Dirksen said. "After all, I know that you've switched bodies with your dog, the President of the United States, an alien, and no doubt others you haven't told me about. And yet you've managed not to tell many people."

"It's not like anyone would believe me," I replied.

"Well, I'm going to tell you about something people just might believe," my teacher said. "And that's why I need your promise that you won't tell a soul."

He pulled open a desk drawer and took out a small tape player with two sets of headphones attached to it. "Do you know what this is, Jake?"

"It's a Walkman," I answered.

"No." Mr. Dirksen shook his head. "This . . . is the mini-DITS. It's the same as the original machine, but I've made it much smaller."

"Cool!" I said. "Does it transfer intelligence or just switch bodies?"

Mr. Dirksen let out a defeated sigh. "It only switches bodies, I'm afraid. I've given up on trying to transfer intelligence."

"No offense or anything," I said, "but it's about time."

Mr. Dirksen handed the mini-DITS to me. "I want you to keep this for the summer, Jake."

"Why?" I asked.

"Kim and I have been invited on a rafting expedition up the Amazon River. It's going to be fantastically interesting but also very dangerous."

Kim was Ms. Rogers, my social studies teacher. She was married to Mr. Dirksen, but she still went by her old name.

"I'm worried that if anything happens to me," said Mr. Dirksen, "the world will never learn about my invention."

"You *want* the world to know about the DITS?" I asked, surprised.

"Oh, yes, absolutely," Mr. Dirksen said. "But not until I've tested this new model. So I want you to take it for the summer. After all," he chuckled, "you should be able to survive camp without much difficulty."

He put his hand on my shoulder and gave me a serious look. "If anything should happen to me, Jake, I want you to carry on my work."

"You mean you want me to be a middle school science teacher?" I asked.

"No, no, not *that* work," Mr. Dirksen said, then pointed at the mini-DITS. "*This* work."

"Uh, okay, sure." I tucked the mini-DITS under my arm. "I promise I'll take good care of it."

"Just remember that the mini-DITS has never been tested," Mr. Dirksen reminded me. "So no fooling around with it."

"You got it, Mr. D," I said.

Mr. Dirksen patted me on the shoulder and walked me toward the door. "So, Jake, are you and your friends going back to last summer's camp?"

"Nope," I said. "I picked a new one this year."

"What's its name?" asked my teacher.

"Camp Gromly or Gramly or something," I said.

Mr. Dirksen raised his eyebrows curiously. "You're not sure of the name?"

"Not exactly," I admitted. "I went through so many camps that I get mixed up. But don't worry, I've got the name written down at home."

3

"What was the Dorkman's urgent news?" Josh asked later as he, Andy, and I walked home from school.

"Uh, nothing," I said.

Josh made a face. "What is this, a secret?"

"So isn't this cool, guys?" I said. "School's over! It's summer!"

"Know what, Jake?" Andy smirked. "That was the lamest attempt at changing the subject I've ever seen."

"Fess up, Jake," Josh insisted.

"Look, it was nothing," I said. "The Dorkman and Ms. Rogers are going on a dangerous expedition to the Amazon, and he just wanted me to promise that if anything happened to him, I'd carry on with his work."

Andy made a face. "You mean, be a middle school science teacher?"

"No, his work on the DITS." I stopped and showed them the mini-DITS.

"Way cool!" Andy gasped. "Does it do the same thing as the DITS?"

"Dirksen *thinks* so, but he isn't sure," I said. "He hasn't tested it yet. He just wants me to keep it safe for the summer."

"You going to leave it at home?" asked Josh.

I shook my head. "And let my sister Jessica find it in my closet? No way. I guess I'll have to take it to camp with me."

"So tell us about this great new camp," Andy said.

I grinned. "It's the only one with its own video arcade."

Josh and Andy stared at me. "You serious?"

I nodded. "And bunks with cable TV and VCRs. And a heated swimming pool. And instead of camp food, every meal is catered by McDonald's."

Josh and Andy both went slack-jawed. "*No way!*"

"Better believe it," I said.

Andy and Josh grinned and raised their palms. We all shared a high five. "Way to go, Jake!"

"There's just one thing, guys," I cautioned them. "If our parents find out what this camp is really like, they could still change their minds at the last minute."

"Good point," agreed Josh. "My parents always talk about how wonderful it is to rough it in the great outdoors. If they find out about the cable TV and fast food, they'll wig."

"So don't say nothing about it," I told them.

"That's a double negative," Andy corrected me. "You should have said, don't say *anything*."

I frowned. "Maybe you're right, but school's over. Forget about English."

"Yeah," agreed Josh. "It's time to start planning our summer of leisure."

4

A week later, early on a Sunday morning, Andy's parents drove us to the Jeffersonville mall. The bus to Camp Grimley would pick us up in the parking lot.

"You think they'll have Night Mission?" Josh whispered to Andy and me in the back of the car.

"What's that?" Andy whispered back.

"This totally cool new video game," Josh explained in a low voice. "You're the head of this platoon sent into the jungle on a night mission. You get to use night-vision glasses and stuff. It's awesome."

Meanwhile, in the front seat, Andy's mom, Mrs. Kent, shifted uneasily. "I feel so guilty about this. We're sending Andy to a camp we know nothing about. I've been so busy I never got around to watching the camp video or calling anyone for references. All we know is that the Shermans and the Hopkas are sending Jake and Josh there."

"If it's good enough for them, it's good enough for us," said Mr. Kent.

"Besides," Andy said from the backseat, "I'll be with my two best friends. How bad could it be?"

"I guess you're right." His mom seemed to relax. "I just feel bad that we didn't do a better job for you."

"Don't worry, Mom," said Andy. Then he gave Josh and me a wink. "Everything's going to be fine."

When we got to the mall, the parking lot was filled with cars. Parents and campers were milling around everywhere.

"Gee," said Mr. Kent, "Grimley must be one popular camp."

"Don't be silly," Mrs. Kent said. "They're not all waiting for the Camp Grimley bus. Buses stop here to pick up campers for dozens of camps."

"How are we going to know where to wait?" Andy asked.

"Over there." Josh pointed to a sign that said "Camp Grimley." The sign was written by hand on a torn piece of cardboard and taped to a light pole. We walked over. No one else was there.

"I guess we're the only ones going from this area," Josh said.

We scoped out the crowd in the parking lot. Each camp had a spot for its campers to gather.

"How come other camps have big, fancy banners and flags while we just have a torn piece of cardboard?" Josh asked.

I motioned my friends to come close so Andy's parents wouldn't hear. "It just shows you how smart the owners are," I whispered. "Instead of wasting money on dumb things like banners, I bet they spent it on totally awesome game systems."

"Then they'll *definitely* have Night Mission," Josh said hopefully.

"Hey, look!" Andy pointed at the entrance to the parking lot where a big, shiny bus was pulling in. "Oh, cool, it's a deluxe motor coach! The kind with the little TVs! I bet that's ours!"

My friends and I watched eagerly as the bus wound its way through the parking lot . . . but then stopped at another camp sign.

Josh's shoulders sagged with disappointment. "Guess that isn't our bus."

"Don't worry," I said confidentially. "Ours will be just as cool."

More buses arrived to pick up campers, but none of them were from Camp Grimley. Even the familiar old green Camp Walton bus showed up. After a while, the parking lot started to empty out.

Mrs. Kent looked worried. "I hope they didn't forget us."

Josh and Andy shot me a concerned glance.

"Hey, it's no big deal," I said. "We're probably their last stop."

Bang! An explosion made us jump. A ramshackle old bus backfired as it trundled into the parking lot, trailing a long white plume of smoky exhaust.

"Oh, no!" Josh groaned.

Andy turned to me. "Don't tell me this is another one of Camp Grimley's money-saving ideas."

I didn't know what to say. The old bus creaked and squeaked as it rolled toward us. Suddenly it veered away and stopped next to a sign that said "Camp Run-a-Muck."

"Phew!" Josh sighed with relief. "I'm glad we don't go to *that* camp."

But the words were hardly out of his mouth when yet another vehicle swung into the parking lot. This one wasn't even a bus. It was an olive-green truck with a canvas tarp over the cargo area — like an Army troop carrier.

The truck stopped right in front of us. A guy with a blond crew cut jumped out. He was wearing a tight olive-green T-shirt and green camouflage pants.

"Going to Camp Grimley?" he asked.

My friends and I nodded, dumbfounded.

"What are you waiting for?" the guy said. "Climb on in. We're movin' out!"

The next thing we knew, he grabbed our backpacks and hurled them into the truck. Then he told us to step up on the back bumper and climb in under the tarp.

"Come on, pork chop, we don't have all day," the crew-cut guy barked when Josh hesitated.

16

Josh climbed in. Andy and I followed. We sat down on a wooden bench. Across from us sat a row of kids.

The crew-cut guy climbed in front and started the engine.

"Excuse me, sir," I heard Andy's mom say outside. "Are you really going to Camp Grimley?"

"Yes, ma'am," the crew-cut guy answered.

"Why aren't they going in a bus?" Mrs. Kent asked.

"I'll tell you why, ma'am," the crew-cut guy replied. "It's because buses are for wimps."

The truck lurched and pulled out of the mall parking lot.

Like it or not, we were on our way to Camp Grimley.

5

In the back of the truck, the two rows of ten campers faced each other with our backpacks piled on the floor between us. Five campers were girls. The rest were boys. We held on tight as the truck bounced and banged along.

Josh glared at me. "If this is another way Camp Grimley saves money for its video systems, they better have Night Mission *Deluxe*."

I didn't answer. This wasn't what I'd expected. I looked across the truck at the campers facing us. "Anybody know anything about Camp Grimley?"

"All I know is my parents picked it for me," said a chubby kid with brown hair parted in the middle.

"My dad said it would be a good experience," added a tall kid who seemed to be all knees and elbows.

"My uncle went there when he was young," said a girl with black lipstick, spiky black hair, and a pierced eyebrow. "He says it changed his life."

A guy sitting at the end of the bench shook his head and smirked at us. He was super-thin, with a buzz cut and a toothpick stuck behind his ear. He was wearing a black T-shirt with the sleeves cut off. On his right biceps was a tattoo of a snake.

"You look like you know something," I said to him.

"I know that by this time tomorrow you guys'll wish you never got on this truck," he replied.

"Why?" asked the tall kid who was all elbows and knees.

"Because Grimley is a survival camp," said the thin kid with the toothpick.

"What's that?" asked the girl with the spiky hair and black lipstick.

"A camp where the only thing you do is try to survive," the thin kid with the toothpick answered. "You have to find or kill your own food. You sleep on the ground and the only running water is what runs in the streams."

"Bull," I challenged him. "I saw the video they sent. How can it be a survival camp if they have cable TV, a heated pool, and the meals are catered by McDonald's?"

"Wait, I saw that video," said the chubby kid with the brown hair.

"See?" I said to the thin kid with the toothpick. "I'm not the only one."

"There's just one problem," said the chubby kid. "That wasn't a video from Camp Grimley."

6

A hush fell over the campers sitting in the back of the truck.

"What do you mean, it wasn't Camp Grimley?" Josh asked the chubby kid.

"It was another camp," the chubby kid answered. "I think it was called Camp Gramerly or something. Camp Grimley never sent a video."

"That's the most ridiculous thing I ever heard!" I sputtered. "You really think I'd be dumb enough to mix up the names of camps?"

Josh and Andy both nodded.

"Gee, thanks for having so much faith in me," I muttered sourly.

"I bet it *is* a survival camp," mumbled the tall kid who was all elbows and knees. "My father always says I'm too soft and I need to get tougher. He'd never send me to a camp with cable TV and a heated pool."

Josh leveled his gaze at me. "Way to go, Jake."

"Wait a minute!" I cried nervously and pointed at the girl with the spiky hair and black lipstick. "Didn't you say your uncle went to Camp Grimley?"

The spiky-haired girl nodded.

"And didn't he tell you it changed his life?" I asked.

"Yeah," said the girl.

"Did he tell you *how* it changed his life?" Josh asked her.

"Not really."

"He must've told you something," Andy said.

The spiky-haired girl shook her head. "That's all he ever says. Just, 'Camp Grimley changed my life,' over and over again. And then he gets this glassy look in his eyes and he starts to shake. And sometimes he even screams. And that's when the nurses come and take him back to the ward for his medication."

"The ward?" Josh repeated with a frown.

"Yeah," said the spiky-haired girl. "You know. The hospital ward."

"How long has he been in the hospital?" I asked.

"Ever since he came back."

"Came back from what?" asked Josh.

"Camp Grimley."

7

It wasn't long before we'd questioned every kid on the truck and learned the following:

1) No one had ever *seen* a video about Camp Grimley.

2) Except for the girl with the crazy uncle, no one *knew* anyone who had ever gone to Camp Grimley.

3) For one reason or another, almost every kid in the truck wasn't surprised that their parents would send them to a survival camp without telling them.

"Okay, so maybe I *did* make a mistake," I finally admitted. "Maybe Grimley is a survival camp. But so what? We're only going for three weeks. How bad could it be?"

Everyone turned to the thin kid with the toothpick behind his ear. Only he wasn't sitting at the end of the bench anymore. He'd stood up and was pulling on his backpack.

"What are you doing?" Josh asked him.

"Bailing," he answered.

"Where're you gonna go?" asked the chubby kid.

"Anywhere," said the kid with the toothpick. "As long as it's not Camp Grimley."

The truck stopped at a light. The kid with the toothpick jumped out and jogged into the woods beside the road.

The rest of the ride passed in silence as those of us left in the truck mulled over what lay ahead. It was midafternoon when the truck turned down a bumpy dirt road filled with rocks and potholes. For the next few hours we bounced and lurched deeper and deeper into a dark green, thickly wooded forest.

"When was the last time we saw another car?" the chubby kid wondered out loud.

"Hours ago," Andy answered forlornly.

"Talk about being in the middle of nowhere." Josh glowered at me as if it was all my fault.

"Let's try to look on the positive side," I said. "We'll probably learn about all kinds of things we never would have learned at the luxury camp. I bet this experience will make us better people."

"Get stuffed, Jake," Josh snapped. "Don't try to sell us on your mistake. You blew it. This is all your fault. End of sentence."

"All I'm saying is that we might as well try to make the best of it," I said.

The truck screeched to a stop and the crew-cut

driver came around to the back. "Okay, pork chops, get out."

We were in a clearing in the middle of the woods. In each corner of the clearing was a medium-size old-fashioned green Army tent. In the center of the clearing was a larger tent.

We climbed out. The driver started tossing our backpacks into a pile on the ground.

"Hey, take it easy!" Josh shouted at him. "I've got a brand-new tennis racket in there."

"A tennis racket?" the driver chuckled. "What are you gonna do with that?"

"Play tennis, what else?" Josh answered.

The driver just smiled to himself and threw another backpack onto the pile.

Meanwhile Andy and I looked around.

"I hate to say this, Josh," Andy said, "but I don't see any tennis courts."

"Gimme a break," Josh replied impatiently. "*This* isn't the camp. There's nothing here. This is just some stopping-off place. We probably have to hike from here."

Just then, the flaps of the big tent in the center of the clearing parted and a man stepped out carrying a clipboard. He looked like he was about our parents' age, only he was a lot more muscular than any of our fathers. Like the driver of the truck, he had a crew cut and was wearing an olive-colored T-shirt and camouflage pants. He was followed by a small group of people who looked like they might have been in college. I had a feeling they were our counselors.

A whistle hung around the man's neck. He placed it in his lips and blew. *Fweeeeet!*

Everyone turned and looked at him.

"If I could have your attention, boys and girls," he said. "My name is Cal McPhearsome and I run Camp Grimley."

He looked down at the clipboard and frowned. Then he looked back at the driver. "Hey, Dewey, how many did you pick up?"

"Twenty, sir," Dewey answered.

"I only count nineteen now," said Cal. "Looks like someone flew the coop. You know what to do."

"Right away, sir." Dewey hurried back to the truck and took off up the dirt road.

Cal McPhearsome turned to us. "In case you're wondering, kids. Dewey's job is to round up any of you who might entertain the notion of leaving camp early. He's darn good at it, too. We've only lost one camper in the past five years. And *no one* ever found him."

He paused and smiled. "Welcome to Camp Grimley."

PART TWO
THE ULTIMATE DRAG

8

The good news was that Andy, Josh, and I were all assigned to the same tent, along with the tall kid, whose name was Jeremy, and the chubby kid, whose name was Martin. The bad news was that our counselor, Ted, was from total weirdness. He was a big, bearish-looking guy with long blond hair halfway down his back. His bushy blond beard and mustache looked like they'd never been trimmed.

He was wearing a green T-shirt with the slogan "Think Like an Animal" on the back. His khaki shorts had extrabig pockets, and his hiking boots were worn-out and battered. In a quiver made from animal skins, he carried a bow made from a stick and some arrows with stone-tipped arrowheads.

"If you're wondering about my T-shirt," he said as he led us to our tent, "it reflects my philosophy of survival in the wilderness. You must become at one with nature. You have to learn to think like an animal."

Walking behind him, Josh rolled his eyes like he thought Ted was mental.

We followed him into the tent. Inside, it was dark and smelled musty.

"Any questions?" Ted asked.

"Yeah," said Josh. "Where do we sleep?"

"Anyplace you want," answered our counselor.

"I don't think you understand," Josh said. "Where are the beds? Where are the cubbies?"

"We sleep on the ground like the rest of nature's animals," Ted replied.

Andy's eyes widened. "On the ground?"

"What about a bathroom?" asked Martin, the short, chubby kid.

"The woods," said Ted.

"The woods?" Josh repeated in disbelief.

"I know we'll be eating dinner later, but I'm really hungry," said Jeremy, the tall kid. "Is there a camp canteen or a snack bar?"

"No snack bar or canteen," said Ted.

"What about a dining hall?" I asked.

"No dining hall," said Ted.

Josh turned pale. "No snack bar. No dining hall. Then what do we eat?"

"After tonight, you'll eat what nature provides," replied Ted. "The other counselors may disagree, but as far as I'm concerned, there's an amazing amount of food in the wilderness. Wild game, and fish from the river. All kinds of berries and roots. And as a last resort, there's always edible tree bark and a wide variety of insects that are very high in protein."

Josh turned to me. He looked ill. "Did he say tree bark and insects?"

I nodded.

"Excuse me." Josh picked up his backpack. "I must be in the wrong place."

He marched out of the tent. Andy and I chased after him.

"Wait!" I said. "I know it's not exactly what we were hoping for."

"Talk about exaggeration," Josh groused.

"It's not really an exaggeration," Andy corrected him. "It's more of an understatement."

"We're not in school anymore, dimwit," Josh grumbled.

As we passed the big tent in the center of the clearing, the flap opened and Cal McPhearsome stepped out. He crossed his muscular arms and blocked Josh's path.

"Going somewhere?" he asked.

"You bet," Josh answered. "I'm thinking like an animal. Like a homing pigeon. I'm going home."

Cal nodded patiently. I had a feeling he'd heard this before. "And just how do you expect to get there?"

"I'll walk if I have to," Josh replied stubbornly.

"It's going to be dark in a few hours," Cal said. "Do you know what happens around here at night?"

Josh shook his head.

"Some pretty nasty critters come out," Cal said. "You've got your snakes, wolves, bobcats, and mosquitoes the size of your fist. Oh, and don't forget about the bears."

Josh swallowed nervously. "Bears?"

"Big bears," Cal said. "Know what we call campers who go out in the woods alone at night?"

Josh shook his head.

Cal grinned. "Grizzly bait."

9

Josh decided not to leave camp after all. A little while later, our tent joined the rest of the camp around a big fire where we ate our last "real" meal of franks and beans.

"For the next two weeks we'll learn everything we can about surviving in the wilderness," said Ted, who skipped dinner and ate carrot sticks and apples instead.

"How come you're having that stuff?" Andy asked him.

"I don't believe in eating processed foods," our counselor answered. "Apples are high in natural fiber, and carrots have vitamin A, which improves your night vision. That'll be important when we get to the Ultimate Challenge."

"The what?" asked Martin.

"You'll see," Ted replied mysteriously.

After dinner, Ted told us to collect pine branches and dry grass for bedding under our sleeping bags. The camp had no electricity and the tent had no light, so we lay in the dark.

"What are we supposed to do at night?" Andy asked.

"Most nights you'll be so tired you'll just want to sleep," Ted replied.

"But tonight we're awake," Josh said. "What about some entertainment?"

"All right," said Ted. "Ever hear of Uncle Remus?"

"Who's that?" asked Jeremy, the tall kid.

"Famous American folktale," answered Ted. "For hundreds of years before the invention of television, people entertained each other by telling stories. The Uncle Remus stories are about Brer Rabbit and his friends, Brer Bear and Brer Fox."

Josh rolled his eyes. "Sounds thrilling."

For the next hour, Ted told us the story of how Brer Rabbit tricked Brer Fox into throwing him in the brier patch. By the time our counselor finished, just about everyone was asleep, mostly from boredom. I was drifting off toward dreamland when Ted quietly got up, took his day pack, and crept out of the tent.

"Where do you think he's going?" I whispered to anyone in the tent who might still be awake.

"Probably to sleep on a *real* bed," Jeremy answered grumpily.

10

It felt like the middle of the night when Ted woke us. The tent was dark and the air was damp and cold.

"Rise and shine, guys, the sun's coming up," he said.

"So?" I yawned.

"Time to get into nature's rhythm," our counselor explained. "For the next three weeks we'll be diurnal animals. That's the opposite of nocturnal. We'll rise and set with the sun. See you outside."

Ted left the tent. When he opened the flap, I caught a glimpse of the dawn's gray light. Then the flap closed and it was dark again. None of us budged from our sleeping bags.

"Shouldn't we get up?" Martin asked.

"Maybe *you* should," Josh grumbled, "but I prefer to make like Brer Rabbit and luxuriate here in my comfortable bed of twigs and grass."

"Ted's going to be ticked off if we don't get up," Andy warned him.

"Ted can go jump in the lake," Josh replied.

"Since there's no lake around here," Andy pointed out, "that's a figure of speech."

"I wish I could figure out how to shut you up," Josh growled.

"I'm going to get up," said Jeremy. "I'm hungry. Maybe they'll have a decent breakfast."

He crawled out of his sleeping bag, pulled on some clothes, and left the tent.

"I'm going, too," said Martin. He got up and followed Jeremy.

Andy was the next to rise. "Might as well get up. I've been lying on a stick all night. It keeps poking me in the back."

He went outside, leaving Josh and me in the tent.

"What're you going to do, Jake?" Josh asked in the dim gray light.

"I hate to say it, but I'm hungry, too," I answered and pushed myself up. Like Andy, I'd had a hard time finding a comfortable position during the night. Sleeping on pine branches and dry grass might have been more comfortable than sleeping on the cold hard ground, but it wasn't a feather bed, either.

"Traitor," Josh griped as I left the tent.

Outside, the day was slowly growing brighter. The girl campers from the tent next to ours were also coming out. They were all wearing shorts and running shoes. One of them was the girl with the spiky black hair and lipstick. We'd learned that her name was Tara.

"Okay, Forest Runners, let's stretch," said their counselor. She was a stocky, blond lady with a crew cut and lots of earrings.

The girls from her tent groaned and exchanged woeful looks, but they started to stretch. Andy and I went over to Tara.

"What's the Forest Runner stuff?" Andy asked her.

"It's the name Morgan gave our tent," Tara answered while she bent down and tried to touch her toes.

"Who's Morgan?" I asked.

"My counselor," said Tara.

"Ready for an easy five-mile run?" Morgan asked the Forest Runners.

"Five miles?" Andy swallowed.

"Morgan says that physical fitness is the key to survival in the wilderness," Tara explained. "Guess that means we're gonna run a lot."

Andy and I watched as she jogged away and joined the rest of the Forest Runners.

"I'm glad I'm not in *that* tent," Andy whispered.

A counselor with thick glasses and a backpack bulging with gear came out of the third tent, followed by a bunch of yawning, bleary-eyed campers. They were all carrying knives or small hatchets.

"Okay, Techno-Wizards," the counselor announced cheerfully. "The first thing we're going to do is hone up on our sharpening skills. Or maybe we'll sharpen up our honing skills."

The campers from his tent groaned loudly to show they thought it was a lame joke. But just the same, they started to sharpen their tools.

"Can you believe they're called the Techno-Wizards?" Andy mumbled as he and I rejoined Ted and the rest of our team. "Is that a dumb name or what?"

"They can choose whatever name they want," Ted explained. "Their counselor, Philip, takes the technical approach."

The flap of the fourth tent opened and out staggered a scary-looking counselor whose long unruly hair was held back by a red bandanna around his forehead. He was wearing a faded denim jacket with the sleeves torn off, black pants, and heavy black boots.

He yawned without bothering to cover his mouth and gave the counselors from the other tents a stony look. Then he spit on the ground and went back into his own tent.

"That guy looks like he belongs in a motorcycle gang, not in a survival camp," Josh quipped.

"So what's his philosophy of survival?" Andy asked.

"Axel?" Ted shook his head. "You don't want to know."

11

Ted told us to sit in a circle and cross our legs. Andy and I frowned but lowered ourselves to the dew-covered ground.

We'd just sat down when Josh came out of the tent rubbing his eyes. When he saw us sitting in a circle he grinned. "Aw, how cute. We're playing our first camp game — duck, duck, goose."

"Have a seat, Josh," Ted replied and then said to the rest of us, "place your hands on your knees. Straighten your backs, close your eyes."

"Why?" asked Josh.

"Because," Ted replied, "we begin each day by meditating on the wonders of nature."

"Talk about wonders," Jeremy said, "I'm wondering when we might get some breakfast."

"Later," Ted answered. "Now breathe deeply through your noses. Relax. Try to absorb the wilderness energy."

Ah-choo! Josh sneezed. "Sorry. Guess I absorbed the wilderness pollen instead."

The rest of us chuckled.

"Focus, boys," Ted said without opening his eyes.

We all sat on the cold ground, meditating.

"Uh, excuse me for interrupting, Ted," Martin said, "but what are we supposed to do with the wilderness energy once we've absorbed it?"

"Don't worry," Ted replied. "Your body will know what to do."

"My body knows it wants to eat breakfast," said Jeremy.

"Mine, too," agreed Andy.

"Hush!" Ted said sternly. "This is serious."

We all got quiet but not for long. Someone's stomach started to rumble. I opened one eye and saw Josh grin. The rumbling grew louder. Now everyone except Ted had opened one eye and was grinning.

"Earthquake!" Josh cried.

Everyone started to laugh.

Ted opened his eyes and looked really annoyed.

"Hey, come on, Ted," Andy chuckled. "It's funny."

But Ted didn't smile. "You won't think it's funny two weeks from now."

12

Ted quit trying to get us to meditate and stood up.

"We go single file," he said and started toward the woods.

"What did you say happens two weeks from now?" Andy asked as we followed him.

"The Ultimate Challenge," Ted answered.

"What's that?" asked Martin.

"A situation where you'll be expected to use your wilderness skills," said our counselor.

"So, it's like a test or something?" I guessed.

"You could say that," Ted replied. "Only it's not like any test you've ever taken before."

"Why not?" asked Josh.

"Because it's a survival test," Ted said.

"What happens if you don't pass?" Martin asked.

"Uh, you have to come back again next year?" Andy guessed.

"In that case, we better pass," said Josh.

Ted didn't say a thing. He just walked deeper into the woods. I noticed that, unlike the rest of us, our counselor walked by placing his toe down first and then his heel.

"How come you walk like that?" I asked.

"It's the quiet way," Ted answered. "To stalk prey."

Behind him, Josh started to prance on his toes like a ballerina. The rest of us clamped our hands over our mouths to keep from laughing.

We came to a brook. Above us, shafts of sunlight streamed down through the breaks in the treetops. It felt good on our skin, but I could hear lots of stomachs grumbling hungrily, mine included.

"I sure hope this leads to a McDonald's," Andy said as we followed Ted along the brook.

"I could really go for pancakes," said Martin.

"With a shake and side orders of hash browns, sausage, and cornbread," added Jeremy.

Ted stopped by a bush and plucked off some red berries. "Try these."

We each put a few in our mouths. Mine tasted sweet but tart. "What is it?"

"Wild raspberries," Ted said. He turned to Josh, who was the only one among us who hadn't tried a berry. "Want one?"

Josh shook his head. "I don't like fresh fruit."

"I feel a lot of negative energy coming from you, Josh," Ted said.

"You can thank Jake for that," Josh answered bitterly.

Breakfast wasn't from McDonald's. It was from the brook. Ted taught us how to make spears from tree branches. Then he started a fire with a bow drill and a fire board while the rest of us waded into the brook and speared fish.

I wasn't a big fan of fish, but by the time we'd caught enough for a meal, the sun was high overhead and I was starving. Everyone ate the fish. Everyone, that is, except Josh.

"I don't like fish," he grumbled.

"No offense or anything, Ted," said Jeremy. "But how come you don't eat normal food?"

"This *is* normal food," Ted replied. "This is what nature provides. The junk *you* eat is abnormal food. It's processed and filled with chemicals, preservatives, and synthetic growth hormones."

"But at least that stuff *tastes* good," said Josh as he finally gave in and nibbled on a little piece of fish.

"You'll be surprised how fast you'll get to like this food," Ted said.

Jeremy took a bite and grimaced. "Sure, when you're starving to death *anything* tastes good."

13

We spent the rest of the day learning how to tie knots, find water, and build a shelter out of pine branches and reeds. As evening approached, we speared more fish and gathered blueberries for dinner.

Tired and aching from the day's work, we headed back through the woods toward camp. We were dirty and hungry, and our hands were scraped and full of splinters.

"I want to go to a different camp!" Josh wailed.

"Try to think positively," Ted urged him. "You're going to stay here and get tough. You're going to learn to become at one with nature."

"I'm already at one with nature," Josh replied. "I just wish I could make like a tree and leave."

Once again, our stomachs were grumbling hungrily.

"Earthquake!" Martin called out.

This time, nobody laughed.

As we got closer to the camp, we could smell the scent of smoke.

"Smells like someone's cooking," Andy said.

"Smells great," I said.

"It's . . . it's steak!" Jeremy gasped. Suddenly he broke out of our single-file line and raced ahead through the forest.

The rest of us gave Ted desperate, pleading looks, but our counselor shook his head.

We reached the edge of camp and were stunned to see the other campers sitting outside their tents eating dinner.

"How come they get real food and we don't?" I asked.

"What you eat is up to your counselor," Ted replied. He pointed at Morgan's tent, where the Forest Runners were sitting around a big pot of spaghetti. Their hair was damp with perspiration and their sweat-soaked T-shirts clung to their bodies. They had obviously spent the day running and exercising.

"Do you realize that spaghetti is made with processed flour?" Ted asked. "And that tomato sauce is full of preservatives?"

"I'd kill for some preservatives," Andy moaned.

Ted ignored him and pointed at Philip's tent. Heavy backpacks loaded with compasses, butane stoves, and orange two-man tents lay on the ground. The Techno-Wizards were eating lumpy-looking foods out of plastic bags.

"They're eating freeze-dried junk," Ted grumbled with distaste. "That stuff is filled with nitrates."

"I'd give my left hand for some nitrates!" Martin cried.

The smell of grilling steaks was coming from Axel's tent. His campers were eating super-rare steaks with bloodred insides. Bright red steak juice ran down their chins as they gnawed hungrily. I wondered what they'd done all day. A tree nearby was covered with freshly gouged initials, and next to the tent lay a bunch of thick sticks that resembled crude baseball bats.

Jeremy was following Axel around, begging for a piece of steak. Axel didn't say a word. He just gave him that stony look. Finally, when Jeremy wouldn't stop begging, Axel pushed him to the ground.

"Hey!" Andy gasped. "Why'd he do that? They've got extra steaks on the grill. They could spare some."

"Axel's not going to share," Ted said.

"Why not?" I asked.

Our counselor just shrugged and didn't answer.

Jeremy trudged back from Axel's tent. "I can't believe he wouldn't give me some steak."

"You don't want that stuff," Ted said. "Red meat's full of cholesterol and fat. Soda's full of processed sugar. All that stuff'll kill you."

"So what?" Josh moaned. "Another two weeks of fish and berries and we'll all be dead anyway."

PART THREE
THE ULTIMATE DECISION

14

"**T**his is the day we've all been waiting for — the Ultimate Challenge," Cal McPhearsome said. "Starting today, only one law applies — survival of the fittest."

It was just after dawn and we were gathered outside our tents. It amazed me how the campers on each team had started to look more and more like their counselors over the past two weeks.

In the misty grayness, Morgan's Forest Runners were all wearing warm-ups and sweatbands around their foreheads. Philip's Techno-Wizards each carried a heavy backpack loaded with gear.

And this was the first time I'd seen Axel's Vulture team up before noon. Like Axel, they were all wearing heavy boots, black jeans, and denim jackets with the sleeves torn off. One of them was Ron, the thin kid who'd jumped off the truck on the first day. As usual he had a toothpick in his mouth and that stony, silent look he'd learned from Axel. We'd nicknamed him Toothpick.

"At noon today your teams will be air-dropped into the wilderness fifty miles from here," Cal announced. "Your job will be to find your way back to camp. The first team that makes it back gets three pizzas with all the toppings they want, plus three big bottles of soda and three big bags of potato chips."

Murmurs broke out among the campers. By now, the Forest Runners were as sick of spaghetti and the Techno-Wizards as sick of freeze-dried scrambled eggs as we were of fish and berries.

"I'd kill for pizza," Josh muttered in despair. I'd never seen him so thin and gaunt. Then again, all of us from the Weed Eaters' tent were thin and gaunt.

"Remember," Cal went on. "Only the winners get pizza. Between now and noon your counselors will announce which of you will go on the challenge. Don't forget, this isn't a game. It's survival. We live in a take-no-prisoners world here. What's our camp motto?"

"Show no mercy!" some of Axel's Vultures shouted. The rest of us were too busy whispering to each other. Josh turned to Ted. "What did he mean, you'll announce who's going on the Ultimate Challenge? Aren't we all going?"

Ted shook his head. "Each counselor takes his best three campers. The others stay behind."

"And do what?" Andy asked.

Ted shrugged. "Whatever they want."

"What about food?" asked Jeremy.

"The camp will supply it," answered Ted.

Josh blinked with astonishment. "You mean, two of us *won't* have to go on the Ultimate Challenge? We can just hang around here and eat?"

Ted nodded. "You'll be left behind. You won't have the satisfaction of putting what you've learned to the test."

Josh looked like he was ready to jump for joy. "Believe me, that's one satisfaction I can live without!"

Ted gave him a frustrated look. "Why can't you have a positive attitude, Josh?"

"I am positive," Josh protested. "Positive that I don't want to go on the Ultimate Challenge! So who's going and who's staying?"

"I haven't decided yet," Ted answered. "I'll let you know."

Then he went back into the tent.

15

The Weed Eaters sat in a circle outside our tent and waited for Ted to make his decision. We were dirty and skinny. Everyone's stomach growled loudly.

"If I have to go into the woods and eat berries for another week, I'm gonna die," Jeremy moaned.

"If I have to listen to Ted tell another dumb story about Brer Rabbit faking out Brer Fox, I'll go nuts," complained Josh.

While we waited, we watched the other teams get ready for the challenge. Morgan's Forest Runners loaded their backpacks with boxes of spaghetti. Outside the Techno-Wizards' tent, Philip gave each of his campers a shiny new compass. Axel's Vultures had gone back into their tent to prepare in secret.

"Everyone else is getting ready, and meanwhile we're just sitting here doing nothing," Andy moped.

"You know what Ted would say," replied Martin. "We should be meditating and becoming at one with nature. That's how he wants us to get ready."

Josh shook his head woefully. "I don't want to go. Cal said two of us wouldn't have to. I'd do anything if he'd pick me to stay behind."

"We all would," Martin said. "Boy, what I wouldn't give to be somewhere else right now."

"Or *someone* else," quipped Jeremy.

In the silent moment that followed, Josh leveled his gaze at me. I could almost see the lightbulb go off in his brain. He pushed himself up.

"Let's take a walk, Jake," he said.

"Where?" Andy asked.

"Nowhere you're going," Josh replied.

"Wait a minute!" Andy gasped. "You're up to something. I can tell."

"Forget it," Josh said. "Jake and I are just gonna talk."

"Not without me, you're not." Andy got up.

The three of us strolled into the woods behind the tents. I already knew what Josh had in mind.

"The answer is totally no," I said.

"Listen, Jake, I've been your friend for a long time," Josh said anxiously. "I've helped you out of some seriously harsh jams. I wouldn't even be here if it wasn't for you. You owe me."

Andy's jaw dropped as he realized what Josh was talking about. "The mini-DITS!"

Shhhh! Josh and I pressed our fingers against our lips.

"You don't want someone to hear, jerkhead," Josh hissed.

"Jake, you can't help Josh and not me," Andy gasped. "If he gets out of going, so do I!"

"I'm not switching anyone," I said. "I don't even know if the mini-DITS works. Dirksen's never tried it on anyone."

"I'm gonna be the first guinea pig," insisted Josh.

"I'll be the second," added Andy.

"It doesn't make sense, guys," I said. "Who are you going to switch with? Who do you know who's definitely *not* going on the Ultimate Challenge?"

Andy's shoulders sagged. "Jake's right. We don't know who's going and who's not. We could switch with someone and still wind up going."

Josh stared off into the woods. A smile slowly crept across his lips. It was the first time he'd smiled since we arrived at Camp Grimley. "There's a way," he said. "And it'll guarantee that neither Andy or I will go."

16

Josh turned to me. "We're not going to switch with anyone. *You* are, Jake."

"Me?" I scowled. "How would that stop Ted from picking you for the Ultimate Challenge?"

"Because you'll switch with Ted," Josh explained. "And then you'll decide that Andy and I aren't going."

"That's right!" Andy cried. "Jake, you have to do it!"

"But if I switch with Ted, that means I definitely have to go," I said.

"So?" Josh asked.

"Why should I have to go if you don't?" I asked.

"You want one good reason?" Josh answered. *"Because this is all your fault!* We wouldn't be at this stupid camp if it wasn't for you. We wouldn't be dirty and hungry and miserable."

"Maybe I made a mistake," I admitted. "But it was an honest mistake. I didn't do it on purpose."

"Doesn't matter," Josh countered. "This is the

only way you can possibly make up for it. Right, Andy?"

Andy nodded in agreement. Deep inside, I knew they were right. It *was* all my fault. If only I hadn't gotten the names of the camps mixed up!

"Okay, I'll do it," I finally agreed. "Or at least I'll try. You guys are going to have to come up with a way to trick Ted into switching bodies with me."

Josh grinned. "Piece of cake."

"Ahem." Andy cleared his throat. "Given the circumstances, I think you mean piece of *fish*."

17

You can't live in a tent with someone for two weeks and not learn a few of his secrets. We knew that when Ted went out for his nightly strolls he always took a Walkman with tapes of a band called Phluke. My friends and I didn't know much about that band, but Martin did because he had a friend who was a "Phlukehead."

"It's like this cult," he'd told us. "They trade tapes of concerts. The New Year's Eve concerts are real favorites."

Josh, Andy, and I went back to camp and into the tent. Ted was inside, sitting cross-legged, still trying to decide who was going to go on the Ultimate Challenge.

"You really have a tape of the 1992 New Year's Eve show?" Josh asked me with a wink.

"Oh, uh, yeah," I said. "I sure do."

"You have it here?" Josh asked, pretending to get excited. "On your Walkman?"

"Yup." I glanced out of the corner of my eye and noticed that Ted was giving us a curious look.

"Oh, man, I have to hear it!" Josh cried.

I went over to my backpack and started to open it.

"What New Year's Eve show?" Ted asked.

"It's nothing," Josh said. "Just this band we like."

"What band?" asked Ted.

"Phluke," Andy said. "Most of our friends think they're lame, but we're really into them."

Ted smiled knowingly. "Well, I've got news for you. There are no tapes of the 1992 New Year's Eve show because there was no New Year's Eve show that year."

Andy and Josh gave me a panicked look.

"Oh, uh, sure there was," I bluffed. "They, er, just didn't play at the regular place."

"You mean, the Ocean Palace?" Ted said.

"Uh, right," I said. "They played, uh, somewhere else."

"That must have been the Seaside Ballroom," Ted said to himself. "But everybody would have known if Phluke played there."

"It, uh, was just for their friends," Josh said.

Ted got up. "I have to hear this."

"Sure!" Josh smiled. "Jake, get out your Walkman."

I took out the mini-DITS.

"That's the strangest-looking Walkman I've ever seen," Ted said. "Why are there two sets of headphones?"

"It's made specially for audiodigital spiritual tape," Josh quickly ad-libbed. "And it comes with two sets of headphones because it's for people who want to share the experience."

"I've never heard of anything like that," Ted said, but he took the headphones anyway. "Still, I have to hear this. I can't believe it's a real tape."

"Uh, you wouldn't mind if Jake listens, too, would you?" Josh asked.

Ted suddenly frowned. "Wait a minute, I thought *you* were the one who wanted to hear it. What's going on?"

Josh turned to me and made another face, as if begging me to come up with an explanation. But this time I couldn't think of one.

"There's just one special part Josh wants to listen to," Andy piped up. "Jake's going to find it for him."

"Oh, okay." Ted put the headphones on.

Josh turned to me. "Well, what are you waiting for?"

I sighed reluctantly and slid on the headphones. Josh picked up the mini-DITS and pushed the button.

Whump!

18

There are some things you never get used to. Switching bodies is definitely one of them. When I opened my eyes I was lying on the dirt floor of the tent. I brought my hands to my face and felt Ted's broad, bushy beard. It was like the time I switched bodies with Santa Claus.

"What is this?" I heard my voice ask. Only I wasn't the one who'd asked it. I looked around and saw Ted in my body staring at his hands.

"We switched you," Josh said.

Usually the people you switch bodies with wig out in surprise and disbelief. But Ted in my body calmly stared across the tent at me in his body. Then he pointed at the mini-DITS.

"I assume this is what switched us," he said.

"That's right," said Andy. "How come you're not totally wigged?"

"Well, to tell you the truth, I've never been a big fan of the human body," Ted answered. "The fact that we can switch sort of confirms what I've believed all along. Can you switch us back?"

"When we want to," Josh said.

"And when will that be?" asked Ted in my body.

"When the Ultimate Challenge is over," Andy informed him.

An odd smile appeared on Ted's lips. "No kidding? And what did I do to deserve this?"

"You never let us have anything decent to eat," Josh said angrily. "Maybe, if you'd let us eat better, we'd be more willing to help you out of this ridiculous situation. But *noooooooooo*, you had to make us eat fish and berries and sleep on the cold hard ground and —"

Ted in my body wasn't listening. Smiling broadly, he turned to me. "Now that you're in my body, you'll have to lead the Weed Eaters on the Ultimate Challenge."

"I know." I nodded sadly and felt Ted's long hair wiggle up and down my back.

"You won't stand a chance," said Ted in my body. "No, I take that back. You have *one* chance. I know secrets — places where you can find food and water, shortcuts, ways to avoid being ambushed. I could write it all down for you."

"Write it down?" Josh repeated, confused. "Why?"

"Because," Ted in my body announced joyfully, "now that we've switched bodies, there's no way in the world I'm going with you!"

19

"**B**ut you *have* to go," Josh insisted.

"Why?" asked Ted in my body.

"Because the whole reason we switched you and Jake was so that he could let Josh and me stay behind," Andy explained.

Ted shook my head and smiled. "Sorry. Maybe *one* of you will stay behind, but not both of you."

Josh turned to me in Ted's body. "Tell him he has to go, Jake."

But before I could say anything, Ted in my body pointed a stern finger at me. "Here's what will happen if you try to take me," he warned in an ominous tone. "As soon as we're in the wilderness, I'll leave you. Don't forget, Jake, I *know* the wilderness. I can live out there for months with just my bare hands. And without me, you won't stand a chance. The only hope you have is to learn my secrets. But I won't tell them to you unless you promise not to take me."

"But if you're so great at living in the wilderness, why don't you want to go?" Andy asked.

"Uh . . ." Ted in my body seemed flustered for a moment. "Er . . . because once we're out there, it's . . . uh . . . a group effort. And there's no way I would want to depend on a bunch of bozos like you."

"Are you *sure* that's the reason?" I asked.

"Sure I'm sure," Ted in my body insisted.

"Talk about negative energy," Josh mumbled.

Ted in my body looked back at me. "I've given you the choice, Jake. Take my secrets into the wilderness and you'll have a chance. Take me and you've got about as much hope as a turtle crossing a highway at rush hour."

I tried to rub my chin and think, but my chin was covered with all of Ted's beard hair. I turned to my friends. "I hate to say this, guys, but it's starting to sound like an offer I can't refuse."

"But that means either Andy or I will have to go with you!" Josh gasped.

"I know," I said.

Josh turned to Andy. "Then *you* should go."

"Why me?" Andy asked.

"Because I won't make it!" Josh cried. "If I have to eat one more meal of fish and berries I'll go straight off the deep end."

"Well, so will I!" Andy shot back.

"Shoot for it, guys," suggested Ted in my body.

"Good idea!" Josh said. "Odds!"

"Evens!" said Andy.

They faced each other and each drew back a fist, preparing to shoot.

"Wait a minute," Josh said. "Let's make it two out of three."

"Three out of five," Andy countered.

"Four out of six," said Josh.

"No, four out of *seven*," Andy corrected him.

"Five out of eight," said Josh.

"Six out of ten," Andy said.

"Seven out of thirteen," insisted Josh.

I turned to Ted in my body. "What about those secrets?"

"Let's go get something to write on," he replied.

"Nine out of seventeen," Andy was saying as we left the tent.

"Ten out of nineteen," yelled Josh.

Ted in my body and I in his left the tent . . . and came face-to-face with Axel.

The Vultures' counselor was dressed in black, with a black bandanna around his head and camouflage paint smeared on his face. He blocked my path and didn't say a word. He just glared at me with that stony expression.

"Uh, what's up?" I asked, nervously.

"Feeling worried, Teddy Bear?" Axel growled.

"What about?" I asked.

"You know what about," said Toothpick, who'd come with his counselor and was also dressed in black. "Axel told us what happened last year. If I were you, I'd quit the Ultimate Challenge now."

"Why?" I asked.

Axel didn't answer. He just glowered at me with that stony look.

"Okay, boys, break it up." It was Cal McPhearsome. "Save it for the wilderness."

Axel narrowed his eyes menacingly at me, then stomped away. I turned to the head of the camp. "What can I do for you, Mr. McPhearsome?"

Ted in my body pulled me aside. "Call him Cal," he hissed. "Remember, you're in my body now."

"Right." I turned to Cal again.

"Time's running out, Ted," Cal said to me. "You have to decide who you're taking with you."

Cal left. Martin and Jeremy were sitting outside our tent, looking pale and scared. They stared at me with fearful eyes, as if dreading the thought that I in Ted's body might pick them to go.

"Hey, don't look like that, guys," said Ted in my body. "It won't be that bad."

"Oh, really, Jake?" Martin answered. "Has Ted told you why Axel's Vultures look more like assassins than survivalists?"

I gave Ted in my body a curious look, but of course he couldn't explain in front of them.

"We won't stand a chance against them," whimpered Jeremy.

"What are you talking about?" I asked.

"Get off it, Ted," Martin replied unhappily.

"Stop pretending that you don't know. This is what the Ultimate Challenge is all about. It's not just about surviving in the wilderness. It's about surviving against your fellow campers as well. That's why they keep talking about how our lives are going to depend on each other. That's why the camp motto is 'Show no mercy.'"

I gave Ted in my body a questioning look.

"Let's go inside," he said.

Inside our tent, Josh and Andy were still shooting to see who would stay behind.

"Once! Twice! Three! Shoot!" They each swung an arm forward and held out one finger.

"Even!" Andy cried. "That's thirty-seven to thirty-four!"

"What are you shooting to?" I asked.

"A hundred and fifty-one out of three hundred," Andy said.

"And no do-overs," added Josh.

"Force field," confirmed Andy, holding back his hand again. "Ready?"

"Ready," Josh said.

"Once! Twice! Three! Shoot!"

Josh stuck out one finger again, but this time Andy stuck out two.

"Odds!" Josh grinned. "Thirty-seven to thirty-five!"

Ted in my body and I huddled in a corner of the tent.

"So what's the story with Axel?" I whispered.

Ted in my body shrugged. "Things got a little nasty during last year's Ultimate Challenge," he whispered back. "And I —"

"Uh, Ted?" Before he could continue, we were interrupted by Martin. "Think I could speak to you in private?"

"Not right now," I answered.

"But it's important," Martin insisted. "I really have to talk to you."

I gave Ted in my body a questioning look.

"Go ahead," he said. "I'll tell you the rest of the story later."

Leaving Ted in my body in the tent, Martin and I went outside. Martin glanced around to make sure no one could hear us.

"Uh, listen, Ted," he said in a low voice. "I know I'm supposed to *want* the Ultimate Challenge, but to be totally honest, I really don't. I'm really scared. I never wanted to come to this dumb camp in the first place."

He blinked and wiped a tear out of his eye. "I mean, I'm scared of the wilderness, I'm scared of the animals, and I'm totally freaked by Axel and those Vultures."

More tears rolled down Martin's cheeks. "I'm sorry, Ted. I'm a wilderness failure. I'm not at one with nature. I'm at one with wimpdom. I wish I wasn't, but I can't help it. I really can't go. I know I'll freeze up. I'm really, really terrified."

He started to sob and shake.

"Hey, that's okay." I put my, I mean, Ted's hand on Martin's shoulder and tried to reassure him. Martin was really bawling now. I could feel him trembling. He wasn't kidding when he said he was scared. This wasn't like Josh threatening to go off the deep end. This was serious.

Martin fell to his knees, clasped his hands, and looked up at me with wet, red-rimmed eyes. "Please, Ted! I'm begging you, please don't make me go! Please! I beg you!"

20

How could I say no? Deep down inside I knew that Andy and Josh would be able to cope with the Ultimate Challenge better than Martin. They wouldn't like it, and they'd probably hate me for the rest of my life, but at least they'd survive. Martin, on the other hand, would probably wig out and spend the rest of his life in a loony bin.

"Okay, Martin," I said. "You don't have to go."

"Oh, thank you, Ted!" Martin wrapped his arms around my knees. "Thank you so much!"

"Ted?" Cal McPhearsome called from the front of the tent. "Ted, you here?"

"Coming!" I called back, and gently eased myself away from Martin.

I went around the tent. Cal was waiting with his lips pursed together pensively. "Take a look." He handed me a white T-shirt. A message was scrawled on it in black marker:

Dear Ted,
I can't do it. Sorry to cop out on you.
By the time you read this, I'll be long gone.
— Jeremy

"He's probably headed out on the road," Cal said. "I've sent Dewey to find him. But the helicopter's due here in half an hour. He won't be back by then."

"So Jeremy can't go on the Ultimate Challenge," I said.

"That's right, Ted," Cal said. "You'll have to choose from the other boys. All the other counselors have picked their teams. It's time you picked yours."

Just then the tent flaps opened and Josh and Andy came out, followed by Ted in my body.

"You cheated!" Andy cried angrily.

"Did not!" Josh yelled back.

"Did too!" Andy insisted. "You held back on the last shot and waited to see what I'd shoot. I formally declare the whole shoot-out null and void!"

"You can't!" Josh shouted. "We agreed no do-overs, force field, remember?"

"That was *before* you cheated!" Andy yelled.

"Face it, Andy," Josh said. "You lost a hundred and fifty to a hundred and fifty-one."

"No way!" Andy yelled. "It doesn't count!"

"What's this all about, boys?" Cal asked.

Josh and Andy instantly clammed up.

Our counselor in my body stepped between them and looked at me.

"So, Ted, have you decided who you're taking?" he asked.

"Funny you should ask that, Jake," Cal said to him. "Ted's just about to tell me."

The time had come. Josh and Andy both stared at me with silent, pleading expressions. Ted in my body narrowed his eyes menacingly.

"Who's going with you on the Ultimate Challenge, Ted?" Cal asked.

I took a deep breath and let it out slowly. "Andy, Josh, and . . . Jake."

21

Josh's and Andy's mouths fell open and their eyes bulged out.

"What!?" Andy gasped.

"Some friend you are!" Josh sniffed.

"Your counselor is not supposed to be your friend," Cal informed him. "He's supposed to be your leader. You should be honored that he chose you for the Ultimate Challenge."

Josh spun toward Cal, and for a moment I feared that he was going to tell Cal exactly how he felt about the Ultimate Challenge. But he managed to hold his tongue.

Meanwhile, Ted in my body gave me a lethal stare.

"Okay, then," said Cal. "It's settled. Now you better get ready. You don't have much time." He moved to the Forest Runners' tent.

As soon as Cal was out of earshot, Andy and Josh got into my face.

"How could you do this to me?" Josh demanded hotly.

"I had no choice," I tried to explain. "I couldn't take one of you and leave the other. It wouldn't be fair."

"Why not?" Andy and Josh asked at the same time.

"Come on, guys, put yourself in my shoes," I said.

"If I was in your shoes I wouldn't even be at this dumb camp," Josh seethed. "I'd be at that luxury camp watching TV and eating Big Macs."

"And playing video games," Andy added with a pout.

"Go in the tent and get ready, boys," Ted in my body ordered.

Josh spun around and wrinkled his nose. "What'd you say?"

"I said, go in the tent," repeated Ted in my body.

The next thing I knew, Josh grabbed him by the collar of his T-shirt. "Let's get one thing straight, wuss. As long as you're in Jake's body, we don't have to listen to you. So bug off!"

Josh gave Ted in my body a shove and sent him reeling backward.

"That's showing him," Andy cheered. "So what do you want to do now, Josh?"

Josh looked around and scratched his head. "I guess we better go in the tent and get ready."

He pushed open the flap and went in. Andy frowned, then went in, too.

That left me, and Ted in my body. Ted glared at me. "I told you that if you picked me I'd leave you in the wilderness."

"I couldn't help it," I tried to explain. "Martin's wigging out and Jeremy ran away. Josh, Andy, and you are the only ones left."

Ted started to rub his chin, then frowned when he didn't feel any beard because he was in my body.

"Fine," he said. "But now that Josh and Andy are going, you might as well give me back my body."

He was right. The only reason I'd agreed to switch was so that Josh and Andy wouldn't have to go on the Ultimate Challenge. But now that they were going, there was no reason for me to be in Ted's body.

Or was there?

"If I give your body back, you'll definitely leave us in the wilderness," I said.

"Uh, no I won't," Ted in my body promised.

"I don't believe you," I said.

Ted narrowed my eyes angrily. "Okay, then I'll leave you *anyway*."

PART FOUR
THE ULTIMATE
CHALLENGE

22

"All right, men, listen up!" Cal shouted above the rumble of the helicopter as it skimmed over the vast and endless green treetops. All four teams were huddled in the open cargo bay of the chopper. As I held on tight and felt the helicopter vibrate, I watched the sun in the sky to our left.

"Each team will get one of these." Cal held up a small gray device that looked like a GameBoy. "It's a Computerized Pinpoint Positioner, or CPP. Your counselor will carry it. It emits a homing beacon so that we can track you down in case you really mess up. Now remember, it's for emergencies only. Your counselor knows that he's not supposed to use it for anything else."

Cal handed out the CPPs. Since I was in Ted's body, he gave one to me. As I put it in my day pack, I couldn't help noticing that when Axel got his, he shared a quick wink with Toothpick.

"We'll be dropping you off in a few minutes," Cal shouted. "Each team will start about a mile apart, but equidistant from the camp. The Vultures go first."

The helicopter slowed down and started to hover over a small clearing. Cal tossed a rope out of the helicopter bay.

"Show no mercy!" each Vulture shouted as he rappelled to the ground.

Axel was the last to go. He turned to me and bared his teeth in a snarl, revealing a glinting gold tooth. "*Hasta la vista*, Teddy Bear," he growled, then grabbed a rope and rappelled out of sight.

The next team off was the Techno-Wizards. Each of them clutched his new compass tightly. The third team to rappel out of the helicopter was the Forest Runners. Finally the Weed Eaters was the only team left.

As we got ready to slide down to the ground, Cal cleared his throat. "I might as well tell you that we took bets last night, and your team is the one everyone expects to come in last. I'd like to think that you'll surprise me, but frankly, I don't see how."

Josh and Andy exchanged a miserable look. Ted in my body just crouched in a corner and sneered at all of us. The helicopter started to hover. We

71

pulled on small day packs with first aid kits in them. Ted in my body was the first to rappel. Then Josh and Andy went. As I grabbed the rope, I turned to Cal.

"Thanks for those words of confidence, sir."

23

I rappelled out of the chopper to the ground below. Andy and Josh were looking around at the thick forest with worried expressions on their faces.

Suddenly I heard a zipping sound behind me. I spun around, but I was too late. Ted in my body had gotten into my day pack and pulled out the CPP.

"This is your last chance," he warned. "Give my body back, and I'll help you guys. Don't give it back, and I'm out of here. And I'm taking *this* with me." He held up the CPP.

"If he takes the CPP, we're toast!" Andy cried. "We'll never find our way back, and Cal won't be able to find us, either!"

"You have to switch with him," Josh urged me.

A voice in my head told me not to do it. "No," I said.

"What?" Josh cried. "Have you gone psycho?"

"Please switch bodies, Jake," Andy begged. "*Please!*"

I shook my head.

"Have it your way," Ted smirked as he stuck the CPP in his pocket. "You know, nature's funny. One minute she's beautiful; the next minute she's filled with danger." He adjusted the straps of his pack. "I'd like to say it's been nice knowing you, boys, but it hasn't." He started to leave the clearing.

"Wait!" Josh cried.

Ted in my body stopped. "What?"

"Take us with you. *Please!*" Josh begged. He pointed at me in Ted's body. "If you leave us here with him, we'll die."

Ted in my body actually pursed his lips as if he was considering it. "Give me one good reason why I should take you."

"Because we're innocent," Josh yelped. "We didn't want to come here, either."

"So?" said Ted in my body.

"So . . . we could help you," Andy said.

Ted in my body scowled. "Help me? How? You're the worst students I've ever had."

"Well, maybe we can't help you *in* the wilderness," Andy said. "But we can help you when you get out."

Ted in my body continued to scowl.

"He's right," Josh said, following Andy's lead. "Like we can help you . . . uh . . . program a VCR."

"And order at the drive-thru window at fast-food places," said Andy.

"And we know all the secret codes to video games," added Josh.

"And how to get gum out of bubble-gum machines without paying," said Andy.

Ted in my body looked at my friends like they were crazy, then he turned away and started into the woods.

"Wait!" Andy yelled.

Again Ted in my body stopped. *"Now* what?"

"At least let us have the CPP," Andy begged.

"No." Ted turned toward the woods.

"Wait!" Josh cried.

This time Ted in my body didn't stop.

"Please take us!" Andy called.

Ted in my body disappeared among the trees.

Josh cupped his hands around his mouth and shouted, "Gee, thanks a lot!"

"Yeah," Andy yelled, "some friend you are."

"I hope you sink in quicksand!" Josh yelled.

"Or get eaten by a bear!" added Andy.

"Or bitten by a snake!" shouted Josh.

"Or . . . all of the above!" Andy shouted.

They stopped and listened. I guess they were hoping that Ted would change his mind and come back.

But all we heard was a bird chirp and the faint rustle of leaves in the light breeze.

Ted in my body was gone.

Josh and Andy glared at me in Ted's body.

"This is all your fault, Jake!" Andy yelled.

"Yeah!" cried Josh. "Now we're gonna die!"

"I'm never gonna learn to drive," Andy cried.

"I'm never gonna get to shave," added Josh.

"Or vote!" said Andy.

Josh made a face. "Who cares about that?"

"Hey, come on, guys," I said. "It's not that bad."

"Are you crazy?" Josh cried. "We're stuck deep in the wilderness about a million miles from everything. We don't have food, water, a place to sleep, or a weapon to defend ourselves against bears and snakes. This is worse than bad. It's the ultimate nightmare horribility!"

Andy frowned. "The *what*?"

"Horribility," Josh repeated.

"There's no such word," Andy said.

"Sure there is," said Josh. "Possible, horrible; possibility, horribility."

Andy shook his head. "No way."

"We can survive this," I said calmly.

"How?" Josh and Andy asked at the same time.

"We just have to stay cool and use everything we've learned," I said.

Josh and Andy looked at each other.

"In that case," began Josh.

"It's even worse than we thought!" cried Andy.

24

"**B**eing negative isn't going to help," I said.

"Look who's talking," smirked Josh. "Inside that hairy body is Jake Sherman, the great outdoorsman. Just because you're in Ted's body and you have a beard doesn't mean you know anything about the wilderness."

"Maybe I do," I said.

"Can you get us out of here?" Andy asked hopefully.

I looked around. The small clearing we were in was surrounded by thick, dark forest that looked as if it had never been disturbed. You could tell by the delicate moss growing on the fallen logs and by the small, frail yellow flowers that would normally be crushed underfoot.

"Amazing," I said in awe.

"What?" asked Josh.

"There's a chance that no human being has ever set foot here before," I said.

"Don't say that!" Josh cried.

"Can't you appreciate it?" I asked.

"Why do I get the feeling this is something we're not going to appreciate for long?" Andy moaned.

"Just tell us which way to go," Josh pleaded.

I looked around. We could go in a dozen different directions. But only one would lead us back to the camp.

"See?" Josh said bitterly. "The great Jake doesn't know which way to go, either."

I pointed into the woods. "That way. South."

"Why south?" Andy asked.

"If we go that way, the sun will be on our right," I explained. "On the flight up here the sun was mostly on our left. The other thing is, it looks like it might be slightly downhill, which could lead us to water."

"That sounds good," said Andy.

"Oh, yeah? Then how come Ted went in *that* direction?" Josh pointed in the opposite direction, north.

Andy bit his lip and gave me a worried look. "How come, Jake?"

"I think Ted went in that direction because . . ." I knew I had to come up with a reason fast, or Andy was going to freak. "Because he was trying to trick us. He figured we might try to follow him back to camp, so he decided to lead us in the wrong direction and get us really lost."

Josh made a disbelieving face. "Bull."

Andy looked like he didn't know who to believe.

"I have to go with my gut feeling," I said. "And that's south."

"I'm going with my *brain*," countered Josh. "And my brain says I'd be totally insane to follow you instead of Ted."

Andy looked back and forth between us. "Come on, guys. You have to agree."

"I think Josh is wrong," I said.

"Well, I think *you're* wrong," Josh shot back stubbornly.

"Oh, great!" Andy cried. "Here I am, a million miles from anywhere with my two nut-brain friends who can't agree which way to go! Why wait to die? Why don't I just dig a hole and bury myself right now? I know why! Because I don't have a shovel. I have to make one! How's that for ironic?"

"Come with me, Andy," Josh urged him.

Andy looked at me. "If I go with Josh, will you come, too?"

I shook my head.

"He's full of it," Josh scoffed. "The second you and I leave, he'll come running after us like a little lost puppy."

"Try me," I said.

Josh wrinkled his forehead and gave me a hard look. "Okay, Jake, if that's the way you want it." He turned to Andy. "Let's go."

Andy still wouldn't budge.

"Listen, guys, we can spend all day arguing," I said. "I'd really like you to come with me, but either way, I'm out of here."

I turned and headed into the woods. In the shade of the trees, the air felt cooler and damper. A second later I heard the crash of footsteps behind me.

It was Andy. "I sure hope you know what you're doing, Jake."

"So do I," I replied.

25

There was no trail to follow. Just brown tree trunks, green underbrush, rotting logs, and gray lichen-covered rocks.

"Hey, wait!" a familiar voice cried behind us as Josh came crashing through the brush. "I can't believe you'd just leave me!"

"We didn't leave you," I said. "You didn't want to come."

Josh chose to ignore that. "This is the wrong way, Jake. I know it is. I can feel it in my gut."

"Then why'd you come?" Andy asked.

"Because I'm a total chicken," Josh admitted. "I'd rather die wrong with my friends than live right and alone."

"We're not going to die," I said.

"Want to bet ten bucks?" Josh asked.

Andy tapped him on the shoulder. "Has it occurred to you that if you win this bet you won't be able to collect?"

"Shut up," Josh grumbled.

It was slow going through the forest. We had to pick our way through the trees, over the fallen logs, and around patches of brier and other thorny undergrowth. Even though it was shady in the woods, we were soon sweating.

"I wouldn't mind something to eat and drink," Andy said.

"How can you think about food at a time like this?" Josh asked in disbelief.

"I'm hungry and thirsty," Andy complained. Suddenly he stopped. "Wait! You guys hear something?"

"Yes," said Josh. "I hear a little voice in my head saying, 'Next time you go to camp, Josh, make sure *you* pick the camp and not that bonehead Jake.'"

"I'm serious," Andy said.

"So am I," replied Josh.

"Hey," I said. "I hear it, too. It sounds like running water."

We followed the sound and came to a stream. After taking long drinks of the fresh, cold water, I suggested that we camp there for the night.

"Why don't we just keep going?" Josh asked. "The faster we get out of here, the better."

"No, Jake's right," said Andy. "It'll be dark in a few hours. If we stop now and make camp, we'll get a good night's rest and be ready to go in the morning."

Andy started to pull off his hiking boots.

"What are you doing?" Josh asked.

"I'm gonna wade into the stream and look for crayfish under the rocks," he said.

"Then I better try to start a fire so we can cook them," I said.

Josh put his hands on his hips. "I guess that means I have to build a shelter."

It took me a long time to make a bow drill and fire board from a stick, a shoelace, and a small chunk of wood, but I finally managed to do it. Then, after about a hundred tries, I actually lit some thin strips of beech bark. By adding bigger and bigger sticks, I got a real fire going.

And just in time, too. The sun was starting to go down.

I was putting rocks around the fire to keep it contained when Andy jogged back from the stream. His day pack was filled with squirmy, kicking crayfish. "Hey, Jake! Check this out! I got dinner!"

By then Josh had finished making a shelter out of pine branches. As it grew dark, we settled around the fire and roasted the crayfish on small pointed sticks.

"What I wouldn't give for some melted butter to dunk these crayfish in," Andy said as he ate.

"What I wouldn't give for a cheeseburger," Josh added with despair.

"Shouldn't we just be glad we've got something to eat?" I asked.

"You're right," Andy agreed apologetically.

"Just promise me," Josh said. "No Uncle Remus stories about Brer Rabbit tonight."

"And let's all pray that a big grizzly doesn't come," added Andy.

No sooner were the words out of his mouth than we heard rustling sounds from the woods.

Andy straightened up. "What was that?"

"Probably just an animal," I said.

The rustling sounds grew louder.

"A *big* animal," Josh said nervously as his eyes darted to the left and right.

"The fire should keep it away," I said, trying to stay calm but feeling pretty nervous myself.

Crack! A branch snapped in the dark. It couldn't have been more than a dozen feet away.

Andy jumped to his feet. "I don't know what kind of animal that is!" he gasped. "But the fire sure doesn't bother it!"

26

Josh and I got to our feet. The rustling sounds were coming closer. What could we do? We had no weapons, no experience fighting wild animals . . .

"Ahhhhhhh!" Andy screamed.

Out of the shadows came . . . me.

"Jake?" Josh gasped.

"Ted," replied Ted in my body.

He glanced around at the shelter, the fire, and the pile of crayfish shells left from our dinner.

"You did this all by yourselves?" he seemed surprised.

"Hey, he's right!" Andy gasped as if suddenly realizing what we'd done. "We've been surviving!"

Josh puffed out his chest proudly. "Yeah, and *you* didn't think we could do anything."

"Right," I said angrily to Ted in my body. "You left us to die."

"So why'd you come back anyway?" Josh asked.

Ted in my body shrugged. "I . . . I couldn't leave you helpless."

"Let me ask you something," Josh said. "When you left us in the clearing, why'd you head north?"

"I . . . I . . ." Ted in my body didn't seem to know what to say.

"You were trying to trick us," I said. "So if we followed you we'd get even more lost."

Ted nodded my head slowly. "I'm sorry. I was angry. I wanted to teach you a lesson."

"Wait a minute! I know why you came back!" Josh cried accusingly. "You realized that if Jake in your body croaked in the woods, you'd never get your body back. For the rest of your life you'd be stuck in Jake's miserable excuse for a body."

"Hey!" I yelled angrily. "That's *my* body you're talking about."

"Is that why you wouldn't give Ted his body back?" Andy asked me.

I nodded.

"No! I, uh, never thought of that," protested Ted in my body.

My friends and I gave him a get-real look.

Ted in my body sighed. "Oh, okay, you're right. I wouldn't want to be stuck in this body. So now that I'm here, can I *please* have my body back?"

I shook my head. "How do we know you won't leave us again?"

"I promise," said Ted.

"That's not good enough," said Josh.

"What else can I do?" asked Ted in my body.

"What can he do for us?" I asked.

"What's the one thing we want more than anything else?" Andy asked.

"I know!" Josh suddenly smiled. "Pizza!"

27

"**Y**ou mean, you want to try to *win* the Ultimate Challenge?" Andy asked.

"Why not?" Josh answered. "We just proved we could survive, didn't we?"

"But what do you want pizza for?" asked Ted in my body.

"We want pizza," Josh began, "because we're not mutants like *you*. We don't get a charge out of eating tree bark and roots and weeds. We want pizza because we're normal. That's why."

Ted shook my head. "I'll be honest. I'd like to help you win, but I don't see how we can. We're too far behind. The other teams have a head start on us."

"Sounds like a negative attitude to me," I said with a wink.

"Yeah," agreed Andy. "If you think we're gonna go through all this and *still* eat fish and berries when we get back, you're mental."

"But the only way to win would be to slow the other teams down," argued Ted in my body. "We can't. We don't know where they are. It would be like trying to find a needle in a haystack."

My friends and I shared a frustrated look.

"Wait a minute!" Josh cried. "There *is* a way we *can* find them!"

"How?" asked Andy.

Josh turned to Ted and held out his hand. "Give me the CPP."

"No!" protested Ted in my body. "You can't have it. You're not allowed. It's for emergencies only."

"This *is* an emergency," Josh insisted. "It's what I call a *food* emergency. This is an If-I-don't-get-that-pizza-someone's-gonna-die kind of emergency. And that someone might just be me."

Ted in my body gave me in his body a questioning look.

"Hand it over," I said.

He took out the CPP and tossed it to Josh, who flicked it on. Andy and I looked over his shoulder. On the screen we could see three glowing yellow dots and one glowing red dot.

"Each of the yellow dots represents one team," Ted explained. "We're the red dot. The closest yellow dot is approximately half a mile southwest of us. It's not moving so that means they've probably settled down for the night."

"What are we going to do?" Andy asked.

"We're going to go on a little night mission," Josh replied with a smile. He headed into the woods.

Ted in my body turned to me in his. "Now that I've agreed to help you guys, can I get my body back?"

"Not until I smell pizza," I answered, and followed Josh.

28

"**T**his is completely against the rules," protested Ted in my body as we snuck through the woods in the dark. Josh was in the lead, keeping one eye on the CPP.

"If you don't shut up, I'm going to make sure Jake *never* gives your body back," Josh threatened.

"Or, at least, not until I've stuffed it with pizza," I said.

"Full of fat hormones and growth chloresterals," Josh added.

"Of course, if I stuff *your* body with pizza then I'll still be hungry when I get back into mine," I mused.

Josh stopped and sniffed. "What's that smell?"

Slight wisps of a strange odor wafted toward us in the night air. I couldn't quite figure out what it was.

"Smoke?" I guessed.

"Smoke and something else," suggested Ted in my body.

"P-U," I said. "It stinks."

"Whatever it is, it means we must be getting close," Andy whispered.

Sure enough, through the woods ahead, we caught a glimpse of some faintly glowing coals, as if a small fire was burning itself out.

"Hey, Mr. Night Vision," Josh whispered. "Can you tell which team it is?"

Ted in my body squinted into the dark. "Uh, I can't see."

"That's because you're not Mr. Night Vision anymore," Josh smirked. "Jake in your body is."

I peered through the dark. "Judging from the running shoes outside their shelter it must be the Forest Runners."

"Good," said Josh. "Then it's time to begin Operation Lace Erase. Come with me, Jake."

Josh led me in Ted's body through the woods toward the campsite. Morgan's team was nestled in a shelter made of pine branches. Their running shoes were lined up outside.

The closer we got, the stronger the odor got. It was one of the most acrid, yucky smells I'd ever encountered.

"What *is* that stink?" I whispered.

"Maybe they burned some green wood or something," Josh guessed.

By now we were holding our noses and wiping tears from our burning eyes.

"Josh," I whispered. "I don't think I can take it anymore!"

"We *have* to!" Josh insisted. "Think of that pizza."

Imagining a pizza with a crispy crust, gooey cheese, and sausage and meatball toppings did the trick. Despite the horrible odor, I followed Josh to the row of running shoes.

"Get the laces," Josh whispered.

As I bent over the first pair of running shoes, the stink was so powerful I could hardly breathe. Suddenly I realized what it was.

Foot odor!

"Those girls probably haven't washed their feet or changed their socks in three weeks!" I wheezed.

"I know!" Josh gasped. "It's a real killer! Grab the laces and let's get out of here!"

A few minutes later, we rejoined Andy and Ted in the woods. Back at our own campsite, we sacked out for the night.

The next morning we were up with the sun.

"I'm starved," Josh yawned as he stretched.

"Me, too," Andy said.

"I'd skip breakfast if I were you," advised Ted in my body.

"Why?" I asked, since in Ted's body I was pretty hungry, too.

"Because if we take time to look for food, we'll never catch up with the other teams," explained Ted in my body.

"He's right," Josh said. "Okay, men, time to move out!"

Andy saluted. "In what direction, *sir*?"

Josh checked the CPP. "South!"

It wasn't long before we came to the spot where the Forest Runners had spent the night. But something was wrong.

"They're gone!" Josh gasped.

"I don't get it." Andy scratched his head. "How could they go anywhere without their running shoes?"

"They wore their shoes," replied Ted in my body.

"What did they use for shoelaces?" I asked.

"Vines." Ted in my body held up a thin, green stem.

"That's ridiculous!" Josh sputtered. "The vines will break."

"Maybe," said Ted in my body. "But if they do, they can just replace them with new vines."

Andy smirked at Josh. "Operation Lace Erase. Great idea, space brain."

"It was better than anything *you* thought up, vacuum skull," Josh shot back.

"Stop fighting, guys," I said. "We better get moving."

We started south again. For a while we followed

the Forest Runners' trail. But around noon, Josh stopped.

"What is it?" I asked.

"I know this is going to sound weird," he said, "but I think the Forest Runners went in another direction."

We all looked at Ted in my body. He nodded. "Very good, Josh. I noticed the same thing a few minutes ago. It appears the Forest Runners veered off."

"Why?" Andy asked.

"My guess is they needed to find water," Ted answered. "That's the problem with Morgan's high-carbohydrate program. It gives you a lot of energy, but it absorbs a lot of water, too."

"Weird," Josh said.

"Not really," replied Ted in my body. "Don't you get thirsty when you eat a lot of bread?"

"That's not what I meant," said Josh. "What's weird is that I don't know *how* I knew that the Forest Runners had turned. I just sort of, er, *sensed* it."

Ted in my body smiled. "You've become at one with nature."

Josh rolled his eyes. "Maybe, but what I'd really like to become at one with is that hot, crusty pizza."

We continued through the woods. Except for our footsteps, there was silence. Here and there, a shaft of sunlight poked through the thick canopy of green above us. I might have enjoyed the scenery if it weren't for the nagging hunger in my stomach and the grungy sensation of needing a shower really bad.

Suddenly the silence was broken by a shout: "Get down on your hands and knees!"

29

The shout had come out of the woods. Was it an attack? Was someone coming?

We stared into the woods in all directions.

"I don't see anyone," Josh said in a low voice.

"Over here!" Ted in my body waved us toward a big, fallen log. As we went toward him we could hear more voices. *Girls'* voices.

"I can't find them!" someone cried.

"Get down on your hands and knees . . . and look!" shouted the voice we'd heard before.

"But it's all yucky and muddy!" cried someone else.

"I don't care!"

On the other side of the big log, the Forest Runners wallowed in a muddy, swampy area. Their arms and legs were covered with dark mud. Morgan was in the middle of them.

"You have to find them!" she shouted at her team.

"Find what?" Andy whispered to us.

"Their running shoes," answered Ted in my body. "The mud must have sucked them right off their feet."

"Then Operation Lace Erase worked!" Josh gasped.

"They'll probably find their shoes sooner or later," Ted predicted. "But this will definitely slow them down."

"All right!" Josh cheered. "That's one team down, two to go. Let's go, gentlemen. Show no mercy! There's a hot, crusty pizza in our futures!"

We started through the woods again. On the CPP we could see the other three glowing yellow dots. One represented the Techno-Wizards, one the Forest Runners, and the other the Vultures.

"Which is which?" I asked as I looked over Josh's shoulder at the CPP.

"There's no way to tell," Ted informed us.

Suddenly one of the yellow dots vanished from the screen.

"What the . . . ?" Josh shook the CPP, but the yellow dot didn't reappear.

"What happened?" I asked.

"One of the other CPPs must have malfunctioned," Ted in my body guessed.

Josh pointed at the two yellow dots left on the screen.

"Then this is the team we'll try to slow down next," he said. "All right, Weed Eaters, let's keep moving!"

Our progress through the woods was slowed by thick underbrush and dense patches of thorny brier. Finally, in the late afternoon, Andy stopped to study some broken twigs.

"I think we're on their trail!" He got down on his hands and knees and searched the ground. "Yup! Here's a footprint! It's the Techno-Wizards!"

"How can you tell?" Josh asked.

Andy pointed at the footprint. "It's a hiking boot, not a motorcycle boot."

"Very good, Andy." Ted in my body congratulated him.

Andy blinked with surprise. "Gee, I guess I really *have* learned some stuff!"

We huddled in the woods. Josh flicked on the CPP. Once again, only two yellow dots glowed on the screen. "This dot must be them."

"I still wonder what happened to the Vultures," said Andy.

"Let's take care of the Techno-Wizards first," said Josh. "We'll worry about the Vultures later."

Just like the previous night, we made camp. Josh and Andy built a shelter, and I started a fire, while Ted looked for dinner.

"I'm starved," Andy groaned as he and Josh collected branches for the shelter. "We haven't eaten all day. I sure hope Ted finds something good."

"What do you think he's going to do?" Josh

asked sarcastically. "Bring back Big Macs and fries?"

"Maybe some more crayfish," Andy said hopefully.

I shook my head. "I hate to say this, guys, but we're a long way from any river. Looks like McBerries and McInsects tonight."

"I can't take it!" Josh cried. "This is gonna kill me! I'd eat just about anything! As long as it was cooked! Lamb brain tacos! Marinated dog! White ant pie! *Anything!*"

"Focus on the pizza we'll win for being the first team to get back to camp," Andy advised him. "Think about becoming at one with that pizza."

But thinking about becoming at one with a pizza wasn't the same as actually *eating* a pizza. Maybe the tinder I was using was damp. Or maybe I was distracted by hunger. Either way, I had a really hard time starting a fire.

"I don't know what to do, guys," I said. "I can't get a fire started."

"Why don't you check Ted's backpack?" Josh suggested. "I bet he has matches."

"No way," said Andy. "Cal would never let anyone use matches."

"I bet he secretly gave them to the counselors," Josh said. "In case of emergency. Just like the CPPs."

"You think?" I asked uncertainly.

"Can't hurt to look," said Josh.

100

I unzipped Ted's pack and stuck my hand in. I was feeling around for matches when my hand hit something long and thin and covered by a plastic wrapper. I pulled it out.

"I don't believe it!" I gasped.

Andy turned and saw what was in my hands. "Beef jerky!" he cried.

Josh spun around. "Where?"

Andy pointed at me.

Half-crazed with hunger, my friends instantly pounced! A split second later, we were in a three-way wrestling match.

"I gotta have it!" Josh cried desperately.

"It's mine!" I yelled. "I found it!"

We rolled around on the forest floor, fighting over the beef jerky. Suddenly Josh pushed Andy away, and he and I got into a beef jerky tug-of-war.

Snap! The plastic wrapper tore in half. Josh and I fell backward. Even before I hit the ground I was stuffing my half of the jerky into my mouth.

"No fair!" Andy cried. "I didn't get any!"

Josh and I didn't answer. We were too busy panting for breath and chewing as fast as we could.

Andy dashed back to Ted's pack. He held it upside down and dumped everything on the ground. Josh and I went slack-jawed as more beef jerkies fell out!

"Aha!" Andy cried gleefully.

Crash! We all dove on the pile.

Once again we were wrestling. "Gimme that!" "It's mine!" "I *need* it!"

It wasn't long before each of us had three or four jerkies. We huddled in opposite corners of the campsite, our cheeks bulging as we frantically devoured the food. I was so busy shoving beef jerky into my mouth that I accidentally ate part of Ted's beard and mustache, too!

"I can't believe Ted had this stuff," Andy sputtered through a half-chewed mouthful.

"Yeah," I agreed. "These things are made from meat. They're filled with nitrates and preservatives. Ted swore he'd never touch stuff like this."

"Well, I've got news for you," Josh said with bulging cheeks. "Ted's a total bald-faced phony."

"No wonder he never complained about the berries and roots," Andy grumbled angrily. "He was probably sneaking these things all along!"

"That environmental hypocrite!" Josh added.

We heard a stick crack somewhere close by.

"Chill, guys," I whispered. "Here he comes!"

My friends and I quickly scooped up the jerky wrappers and stuffed them in our pockets. A moment later, Ted in my body came out of the woods.

"Bad news, guys." He looked grim. "All I could find was some roots and tree bark. It won't make much of a meal."

My friends and I nodded in mock sympathy.

"Sometimes you just have to go hungry," I said.

"The important thing is to stick to your beliefs," added Josh.

"You can't forget about the big environmental picture," added Andy.

Ted in my body nodded. "I'm glad you guys understand. In the long run it'll make the world a better place. And you'll be better human beings."

"Like you, Ted?" Andy asked innocently.

"I try," Ted replied earnestly. "That's all anyone can do."

"Oh, yeah?" Josh held up an empty beef jerky wrapper. "Maybe there is something else you can do. You can talk like a righteous environmentalist Save-the-Earth vegetarian and then sneak off at night and eat beef jerky while the rest of your team starves."

Ted in my body turned pale. "You . . . you didn't happen to leave *just one* for me, did you?"

My friends and I grinned and shook our heads.

30

I can't say we enjoyed watching Ted in my body eat roots and tree bark for dinner. In fact, it was kind of pitiful. He admitted that while he sincerely *believed* it was wrong to eat meats and processed foods, he found it impossible to live that way.

"I mean," he said, "in a perfect world, we'd all be better off if we ate less red meat and more vegetables."

"Right," agreed Josh. "And in a perfect world we never would have come to this crazy camp in the first place."

"Know what, Ted?" Andy said.

Ted stiffened, as if he expected Andy to criticize him.

"Now that I know you're not perfect," Andy said, "I like you better."

Josh and I nodded in agreement.

"In fact," Andy continued, "I feel bad that we ate all your beef jerky and didn't leave you some."

Ted in my body actually looked like he was blinking back tears. He turned to Josh and me. "You mean it, guys?"

Josh and I glanced at each other. I'm not sure either of us would have gone *that* far. But we gave him halfhearted nods anyway.

Ted bit into a piece of bark and started to chew. "Know what, guys? I've had campers with better wilderness skills than you, but I've never had campers with more heart. How about a group hug?"

My friends and I traded wary looks.

"Maybe another time," Josh said.

"Yeah," agreed Andy. "Let's not go overboard."

Shortly after sunset we mobilized Operation Compass Swipe.

"Without their compasses those guys will be helpless," Josh whispered as we snuck through the dark woods and hid behind the trees just outside the Techno-Wizards' camp. It wasn't long before the Wizards finished dinner and crawled into their shelter. Moments later we could hear them snoring.

"They must be really tired," Andy whispered.

Josh turned to Ted in my body. "Okay, Mr. I-Never-Touch-Red-Meat. Go in there and take their compasses."

Ted in my body crept off silently. It was spooky how noiselessly he could sneak through the woods and into their shelter.

105

A moment later, he returned with the compasses. We started back through the dark to our camp.

"That's two teams down and one to go," Andy said. "All we have to do now is slow down the Vultures and that pizza dinner is ours."

Suddenly Ted in my body froze. We quickly saw why. Someone was sitting at our campfire, roasting a marshmallow on a stick.

It was Axel!

He looked up at us and bared his teeth. The light from the fire's flames reflected off his gold tooth. "Did I hear someone say something about slowing down the Vultures?"

We heard sounds behind us. The rest of the Vultures came out of the dark forest. They were carrying wooden clubs.

31

Tapping the clubs against their palms, the Vultures stepped toward us. My friends and I formed a tight circle with our backs pressed together.

Meanwhile, Axel slowly pushed himself up. "Know what's funny?"

"Uh, a two-hundred-pound parakeet named Hank?" Andy guessed.

"No, dummy," Axel grumbled. "I meant about you guys sabotaging the Forest Runners and the Techno-Wizards."

"What?" asked Ted in my body.

"I thought the Vultures were going to have to do all that work," said Axel. "But you guys made our job easy. You did it for us."

"Well, uh, then I think it's only fair that we all share the pizza dinner," I said.

Axel frowned at me. "Since when do *you* eat pizza, Teddy Bear? I thought you only ate moldy bean sprouts and caterpillars."

"Er, I was thinking about my team," I quickly replied.

Axel grinned. "Well, ain't that cute. The trouble is, I'm thinking about *my* team. And I happen to know that none of them wants to share their pizzas with a bunch of weed-eating wimps."

"That's alliteration!" Andy said brightly.

"Shut up!" Axel yelled at him.

"So what are you going to do to us?" Josh asked.

Axel scratched his head. "Good question."

"We could tie 'em all to a tree and leave 'em for the wolves," suggested Toothpick.

My friends and I exchanged frightened looks.

"At least it's not the brier patch," mumbled Ted in my body.

"What'd he say?" asked Axel.

"Something about a brier patch," another Vulture answered with a shrug.

"Maybe we could shove 'em in a bear cave and block it up behind them," suggested the fourth Vulture.

"Even *that* would be better than the brier patch," sighed Ted in my body.

Axel turned toward him. "What's with you and this brier patch?"

"Nothing!" Ted in my body gasped fearfully.

"How about we tie 'em up and set 'em adrift on

a raft on a lake?" suggested Toothpick. "Then the alligators'll get 'em."

"There are no alligators around here, stupid," Axel snarled. "Besides, I know what we're gonna do. Follow me."

32

Using a flashlight, Axel and his Vultures led us through the dark woods.

"I thought flashlights weren't allowed," I said.

"Don't talk," Axel said.

"Where are you taking us?" Josh asked nervously.

"Be quiet," Axel ordered.

"You guys aren't playing by the rules," Andy complained.

"Shut up!" Axel shouted.

Andy gave me a terrified look. All the horribilities of what we were about to face flitted through my mind — a snake pit, quicksand, a bear den. My heart started to beat hard and my mouth went dry. This was probably it. The end of my life. Just as I'd feared, we were all going to perish in the wilderness. And all because I'd gotten the stupid name of the camp mixed up!

Ahead of us, Axel stopped and swept the flashlight beam over a thick patch of overgrown green vegetation.

"What is it?" asked Toothpick.

"It's a brier patch, dummy," Axel answered. "See all those thorns and stickers?" With a nasty grin he turned to Ted in my body. "I bet this is the *last* thing you wanted to see, right, Jake?"

Suddenly I realized why Ted in my body had been dropping hints about the brier patch. That was exactly how Brer Rabbit tricked Brer Fox!

Meanwhile, Ted in my body pretended to tremble. "Don't!" he begged hoarsely. "Not the brier patch! Please, anything but *that*!"

Axel just kept grinning. "Tough luck, pal." Then he turned to his team. "Throw 'em in, guys."

33

"Ow, OW, *OW!*" Andy cried in the dark. "This hurts!"

"Yikes!" screamed Josh. "Ouch!"

They'd thrown all of us in the brier patch. Sharp thorns and prickles were sticking into my body in a thousand different places. Meanwhile, the Vultures were laughing and patting each other on the back.

"Way to go, Axel!"

"That'll slow 'em down."

"Okay, dudes," Axel said. "Let's get back to that nice shelter the Weed Wimps were so kind to build for us. We'll get some sleep and head out in the morning. By tomorrow night we'll be chowing down on a big pizza dinner."

The Vultures disappeared into the dark woods, leaving us in our prison of briers.

"Guys, you okay?" whispered Ted in my body.

"Are you *crazy?*" cried Andy. "How could we be okay? We're getting stuck all over!"

"Why'd you want Axel to throw us in this stuff?" Josh wailed.

"It worked for Brer Rabbit," replied Ted in my body.

"Well, we're *not* rabbits, okay?" Josh cried. "We weren't born *or* bred in a brier patch. And right now we're in total pain."

"Keep your voice down," I hissed.

"Drop dead, Jake," Josh muttered. "This is all your fault. If it wasn't for you we wouldn't be in this mess."

"Will you give that up already?" I shot back. "I've told you a hundred times I'm sorry."

"It's not enough," Josh yelped. "Sorry doesn't get the thorns out of my butt."

"I hate to bring this back to reality," interrupted Andy, "but does anybody know how to get out of this stuff?"

"Just follow me," said Ted in my body.

"Follow you?" Josh cried. "I can't even *blink* without getting stuck by a million thorns. How am I supposed to follow you?"

"Just do it!" I hissed.

Moaning, groaning, and frequently yelping with pain, we followed Ted in my body out of the brier patch. Finally we reached a small clearing. The moonlight glistened on the little drops of blood seeping out of our scratches.

"I'm bleeding all over!" Andy moaned.

"We all are," replied Ted in my body. "But they're minor cuts and scratches. They won't stop us."

"Stop us from what?" I asked.

"From getting our revenge," Ted grumbled.

34

We spent most of the night bending young trees over until they were nearly looped double. Then we tied snares to their tops. It was hard work in the dark and we didn't finish until early morning. By then, the sky was turning gray with dawn. We were bleary, tired, and hungry.

"How many snares do you think we set?" Josh asked.

"At least thirty," answered Ted in my body. "Maybe more."

"I just hope I can remember where they all are," Andy said with a yawn.

"Boy, I'm so hungry I could eat a pizza all by myself," Ted in my body groaned.

My friends and I stared at him in shock. "What'd you say?"

Ted in my body blinked with astonishment. "I, uh, I didn't mean it, I swear! All I want is a nice, juicy apple!"

Andy, Josh, and I shared a wink. "*Sure*, Ted."

We hid behind the trees and waited for the Vultures to wake up. Ted in my body was hiding near me.

"Hey, Ted," I whispered. "You never told me what happened last summer that made Axel so mad."

"I told him he had the brains of a rock," Ted in my body whispered back.

"That's *all*?" I asked.

"He's very sensitive about stuff like that," Ted in my body replied.

It wasn't long before the Vultures crawled out of their shelter and started into the forest. It was obvious that they were eager to get back to camp and enjoy that pizza dinner.

As they came through the woods toward us, I stepped out from behind a tree. "Hey, Axel, you big dork!"

Axel's jaw fell when he saw me. "Ted? How'd you get out of the brier patch?"

"Slowly," Andy yelled and stepped out from behind another tree. "And with a lot of pain, thanks to you, you dumb jerk!"

Axel's eyes narrowed angrily.

"But it's okay," Josh added as he stepped out from behind a third tree, "because now we're going to beat you hairy lard-brains back to camp. You can watch us eat pizza tonight."

Axel turned to the rest of the Vultures and shouted, "Get 'em!"

The Vultures thrashed through the woods toward us. We Weed Eaters immediately spread out and headed toward the tree snares we'd set during the night. Axel was coming after me as I wove a crooked course through the snares.

Sproing! I heard a snare trip somewhere in the woods. That meant one Vulture was caught.

Sproing! Sproing! I counted two more.

Sproing! That was it! Four *sproings* meant Axel and his Vultures were all caught!

I stopped and turned around.

Just as I expected, two of the Vultures were now hanging upside down from the tops of trees, flailing their arms in a vain effort to get free.

I heard more thrashing sounds and looked in another direction, expecting to see Axel and Toothpick also hanging from trees.

But I was in for a surprise.

35

Instead of finding Axel and Toothpick hanging upside down from trees, I found Ted in my body and Andy!

"What happened?" I gasped.

"I *told* you I couldn't remember where all the snares were," Andy answered miserably.

I turned to Ted in my body. "You're supposed to be the expert at this stuff! What's *your* excuse?"

"I just couldn't stop thinking about that pizza," he moped.

If Ted in my body and Andy were hanging from trees, that meant Axel and Toothpick were still on the ground.

Meanwhile, the only free Weed Eater besides me was Josh. I looked around, but all I saw was woods.

"Josh!" I called. "Where are you?"

"Over here." Josh stepped out from behind a tree.

"Come on!" I yelled. "You have to help me get our guys down."

"Think again, Weed Wimp," a voice snarled.

I spun around. Axel and Toothpick were standing behind me, holding wooden clubs.

"You're not getting anyone down," Axel growled as he slapped the club against his palm. "Because you're about to become roadkill."

In the tree where he was hanging upside down, Andy cleared his throat. "Uh, excuse me, but he can't become roadkill if there are no roads around here."

Axel ignored him and nodded to Toothpick. "You get the one with the red hair," he said, meaning Josh. "I'll get Teddy Bear."

They started toward us. I glanced nervously at Josh. We had no weapons and no training in hand-to-hand combat.

"What are we gonna do?" I asked.

"I don't know about you, but I know what I'm going to do." Josh turned and stepped into the nearest unsprung snare.

Sproing! He shot up into the tree and hung there upside down.

"Why'd you do that?" I cried.

"Because it beats getting turned into roadkill," Josh answered.

"He's right." Axel turned his nasty grin toward me. "Now it's two against one, Teddy Bear. Your friend just made our job a whole lot easier."

36

I took off through the woods. There were more snares, and hopefully Axel and Toothpick didn't know where they were.

Sproing! I heard another snare go off behind me. Looking around, I saw Toothpick shoot into the air and hang there upside down, flailing.

"Very good, Teddy Bear!" Axel yelled behind me. "Now it's just me and you."

"Actually it's *you* and *me*," Andy called in the distance.

Luckily Ted's body was in good shape, and I managed to stay ahead of Axel in the woods.

"What's the point of running, Teddy Bear?" Axel called behind me. "It's not gonna help get your team back to camp any sooner. Your only choice is to stop and fight."

He was right. As long as the rest of the Weed Eaters were hanging from the trees, we couldn't win. On the other hand, I didn't see how I could win in a fight with Axel.

But I stopped running anyway. "Okay, Axel, I'll fight you."

"You will?" Axel looked surprised.

"I just need some time to psych myself up," I said.

Axel gave me a suspicious look. "Is this a trick?"

"No way," I said. "All I want to do is go back to the shelter and listen to a tape."

Axel frowned. "What kind of tape?"

"Uh, self-help," I replied.

"Self-help for *fighting*?" Axel scowled.

"Sure," I said. "Why not?"

Axel scratched his jaw and thought. "Well, okay. But I'm coming with you."

37

We went back to the shelter. By now, the fire from the night before had burned out. All that was left was a ring of rocks around a heap of cold, gray ashes.

I sat down and took the mini-DITS out of my day pack.

Axel smirked. "You really think listening to some tape is gonna help you in a fight?"

"It's the only chance I have," I answered.

"If that's your only chance, you're out of luck, sucker." Axel chuckled meanly.

In desperation I slipped on the mini-DITS headphones. What could I do to beat Axel? What would Ted do? What would Uncle Remus have Brer Rabbit do?

I had an idea. Adjusting a dial on the mini-DITS, I pretended to turn up the volume.

I began to chant: "Murder. Maim. Kill."

I jumped to my feet and started to pump myself up, grunting "Kill! Massacre! Destroy!"

Clenching my fists and curling my arms like the Incredible Hulk, I gritted my teeth and made my eyes bulge. "Kill! KILL! *KILL!*"

Out of the corner of my eye I watched Axel scowl at first and then begin to look worried.

"KILL! KILL! KILL!" I screamed.

Axel jumped up. "What the heck are you listening to?" He grabbed the other set of headphones and pulled them on.

This was my chance! I quickly looked around for something to switch Axel with. But there was nothing!

Just the dead ashes from the fire, and the rocks, and the shelter, and —

Wait a minute!

Some of those rocks were about the same size as a human head!

"I don't hear nothin'." Axel adjusted the headphones. "What is this?"

I yanked off my headphones and jammed them down on one of the head-sized rocks.

"What the . . . ?" Axel grunted.

I pushed the button on the mini-DITS.
Whump!

38

"What happened?" asked Ted in my body as I cut the snare that was holding him up in the tree.

"I remembered that you said Axel had the brains of a rock," I said.

"So?"

"I guess you weren't kidding." I moved on to Andy's tree and helped him down.

A few minutes later, my friends and I were back at the shelter. Axel was standing exactly where I'd left him with a stony expression on his face. He hadn't moved an inch.

Ted in my body looked down at the rock with the headphones on it. He winced. "You switched him with a *rock*?"

"Not a lot of difference as far as I can see," Andy commented with a shrug.

"He just doesn't move as much," added Josh.

"Now what?" asked Ted in my body.

Toothpick and the other Vultures were still

hanging from the trees. They were shocked when we cut them down and told them we wanted to share the victory pizza dinner with them.

All they had to do in return was help Josh and me get Axel and the rock back to camp. Then I gave Andy the Forest Runners' shoelaces and the CPP and told him to go find them and give them their shoelaces back. I did the same thing with Ted in my body and the Techno-Wizards' compasses.

"We'll all meet in the woods outside the camp just before dinnertime," I said.

Ted in my body started into the woods, then stopped. "Wait a minute," he said. "Can I have my body back now?"

"Not yet," I said.

39

Just before dinner we met the other teams in the woods outside camp. Philip, the head of the Techno-Wizards, and Morgan, the head of the Forest Runners, looked puzzled.

"I don't get it, Ted," Morgan said to me. "Why'd you help us? Now the Weed Eaters won't win."

"Yes, we will," I said.

We lined up by teams with the Weed Eaters in front and marched back into camp.

Cal was waiting for us in front of the big tent. His arms were crossed and he was nodding slowly.

"Very interesting, Ted," he said.

"How come you're not surprised?" I asked.

Cal held up a CPP. "I've been following the team movements since the beginning. I have to admit that it was pretty confusing at first. But in the end I figured it out. Your Weed Eaters managed to surprise me after all."

"We were the first back to the camp," I said.

"That means we get the pizza dinner. Only we're going to share it with the rest of the teams."

"That means you'll each get a lot less," Cal warned me.

"Yeah," I said. "That's exactly what it means."

40

"**I** can't believe you guys came in first," Martin said later as we sat around a big campfire, eating pizza.

"How come you helped the other teams, Ted?" Jeremy asked.

I was still in Ted's body. "Because, like Cal said, this isn't a game. It's survival. And surviving isn't about beating your fellowman. It's about helping everyone make it."

"I thought it was about being at one with nature," said Martin.

"Yeah, that's important," I agreed. "But what's *really* important is being at one with other human beings." I held up a hot crusty slice with sausage and meatball toppings and took a big bite. "And eating pizza on a regular basis."

41

After dinner, Ted and I switched back to our old bodies. Ted admitted that the pizza, chips, and soda were the best things he'd tasted in years.

"I guess I'll have to make an exception for them once in a while," he said.

We switched Axel and the rock, too. The funny thing was, nobody noticed the difference.

The next morning, Ted hung out with us while we packed up for the trip home.

"Guys, I have to admit," he said with a smile, "that you got a lot closer to nature than I ever expected."

"You're telling me," Josh replied. "If I don't take a shower and wash all this dirt off soon, stuff's going to start growing on me."

"Is there anything else you want to admit?" Andy asked our counselor.

"Well, I wouldn't mind if you gave me some of those secret video game codes you mentioned," Ted said.

Martin and Jeremy went up to Ted.

"Thanks for not picking me to go on the Ultimate Challenge," Martin said.

"And I'm sorry I ran away," added Jeremy.

"Really?" Ted asked.

"Well, no." Jeremy grinned. "But I figured I'd say it anyway."

Ted turned to Andy and me. "Do you feel like you learned anything?"

"I learned that when the going gets tough, the tough go shopping," said Andy.

"And if I ever grow a beard," I said, "I'll try not to eat it."

Later, Dewey drove us home in the truck. When we got back to the Jeffersonville mall, our parents were all waiting for us.

"You've lost weight!" Mrs. Hopka gasped when she saw how skinny Josh was.

"Hey, what do you expect?" Mr. Hopka chuckled. "He's been trying to live on camp food."

"You're so dirty!" Mrs. Kent sounded alarmed when she saw Andy.

"Big deal," scoffed Mr. Kent. "I never washed when I went to camp, either."

"Did you have fun?" my mother asked me.

"Of course he did!" exclaimed my father before I could answer. "Summer camp is *always* fun. I bet you boys can't wait to go back next year. Am I right?"

My friends and I traded a doubtful look.

"Know what's weird?" said Andy. "Now that it's over, in a strange way I'm sort of glad we did it."

"You mean, because we learned stuff we probably never would have learned at a camp with video games and food from McDonald's?" I guessed.

Andy and Josh nodded.

"Does that mean we might actually want to go back to Camp Grimley next year?" I asked.

Andy looked at Josh. Josh looked at me. I looked at Andy. All at once we shouted, "No way!"

ABOUT THE AUTHOR

Todd Strasser has written many award-winning novels for young and teenage readers. Among his best-known books are *Help! I'm Trapped in Obedience School* and *Abe Lincoln for Class President*. His most recent books for Scholastic are *Help! I'm Trapped in Obedience School Again* and *Help! I'm Trapped in an Alien's Body*.

Todd speaks frequently at schools about the craft of writing and conducts writing workshops for young people. He and his family live outside New York City with their yellow Labrador retriever, Mac.

You can find out more about Todd and his books at http://www.toddstrasser.com